Islands of
Cedars

A NOVEL BY
Shana Smith

Published by St. Petersburg Press
St. Petersburg, FL
www.stpetersburgpress.com

Design and composition by St. Petersburg Press
Cover Art by Judi Cain – https://www.judicain.com
Cover design by St. Petersburg Press and Isa Crosta

Print ISBN: 978-1-940300-59-7
eBook ISBN: 978-1-940300-60-3

First Edition

5% of all net profits from the sale of this book will be donated to the Rosewood Heritage Foundation.
To make a donation, please visit
www.RememberingRosewood.org

DEDICATION

THIS BOOK IS dedicated to the memory of my father, Dr. Albert C. Smith:

When we first moved to Gainesville, Florida from Hawaii in 1981, my marine biologist dad did not realize that Gainesville was so far from the ocean. As a native Californian, the son of immigrants, and the first in his family to earn a college degree, he then went on to graduate school for a Ph.D. in marine biology followed by medical school for an M.D. in clinical pathology. He then worked as a professor in Hawaii for many decades. He was never far from saltwater. Gainesville, even with all of its stunning natural wilderness, was too far inland for him, so he looked on a map, found a road that was a straight shot to a town on the Gulf of Mexico called "Cedar Key," and announced we were all going there. Barely a teenager, I remember thinking what a long drive the fifty-five miles between Gainesville and Cedar Key was, and how brown and strange and calm and bathwater warm the Gulf water was compared to the wild cool Pacific.

But my dad was in love. Cedar Key is an estuary, a rare and fabulous entity for a marine biologist, and one almost unheard of to us Pacific folks. He soon showed me why this tannin-rich, mysteriously murky water was a wonder: it literally teemed with life, as it was a nursery for hundreds of diverse species. Soon, we became a part of Cedar Key, at first going every weekend and eventually living in a little house by the cemetery for as many days as we could manage each week between his job at University of Florida and the VA Hospital and our school schedules. I spent most of the weekends, summers, and holidays throughout my teen years out on the open Gulf, or cast netting barefoot on the dock, or snorkeling the shallow seagrass beds in search of sea stars, or combing the sandbars for quahogs and sand dollars. In college, I got to live out at the Seahorse Marine Lab in the Cedar Keys National Wildlife Refuge for weeks and sometimes months at a time, spending hours on an outboard combing every inch of the island.

In Hawaii, the hukilau–catching fish by nets–is part of every-day life. In Cedar Key I became an expert cast netter, trained by the late Captain Throckmorton to read the tides and land the best fish right from the old wooden dock. My dad loved to take out the beach seine and my job would always be to serve as his anchor near the shore. He would do the stingray shuffle all the way out to the boat channel, and because the water was so shallow, he looked like a little dot out there on the water. So I nicknamed him "Pop-the-Dot." The locals just called him "Doc." Once he reached the channel, Pop-the-Dot would pull the net around in a semi-circle and head back to shore. I would pull the other side, and together we'd inspect the haul: mullet, catfish, grunts, redfish, whiting, snook, pinfish, and many more species of fish. We also pulled up rocks and oyster clumps filled with invertebrates like sponges, corals, seahorses, octopi, and a million other treasures. We would take some creatures home for our many aquaria and his research on marine animal pathology and human systems modeling, and throw back the rest.

We spent endless summers adventuring together in Cedar Key well into my early adult years, usually starting our days by sharing breakfast at the old Johnson's restaurant overlooking the wooden pier. When we moved to St. Petersburg, we continued the tradition and ate breakfast every Sunday morning at the Friendly Fisherman Restaurant over the wooden boardwalk at Hubbard's Marina while watching the head boats load up some serious rods and bait for a day or three out on the Gulf. In the evening, we'd come back to the marina to greet them, ready to collect fish eye lenses from the fileted carcasses for Pop-the-Dot's research. I even worked as a mate for a couple of years on both head boats, the Friendly Fisherman and the Florida Fisherman, and earned a one-hundred-ton captain's license along the way, much to my father's pride.

Even though we had the full bounty of the Gulf right there at John's Pass, he would get a yearning for Cedar Key every couple of months. I knew we were about to make the trip when he would wistfully start talking about getting a palm salad at sunset at the Seabreeze restaurant, or taking an outboard over to Seahorse Key for some species collecting and shooting the breeze with the ranger and the lighthouse keeper. Time didn't move as quickly in Cedar Key, he would often note. He liked that.

When I left my Ph.D. program in Biological Oceanography at the University of South Florida to pursue a career in children's music, we had a falling out. He kept hoping that I would go back and finish my doctorate, that our years of boating, netting, snorkeling, species sampling, and oceanographic adventures together would continue into the future, and I would just play music and write as a pleasant hobby. One day, missing the carefree days spent with him on, in, and around the ocean, I exclaimed, "Pop, I know this isn't the path you'd envisioned for me, but I wish you would stop asking me when I will go back and finish my Ph.D. and start my life as a marine scientist. I loved it, but I also love playing music and writing. Please, Pop-the-Dot, can you please just be proud of me, just the way things are?"

From that day forward and until our last conversation before he went into a coma, he ended every phone call, every get-together, and sometimes every sentence with: "Shana Banana, I am so PROUD of you!"

Pop-the-Dot passed away way too early, from heart failure, at the age of sixty-nine. And no wonder. From his early dysfunctional days as a Jewish kid in the Los Angeles slums until his last years as a pioneering marine scientist and medical doctor in his beloved Cedar Key, his heart held both deep, unresolved trauma and tremendous love, and the weight of these two opposing forces was overwhelming.

He died less than three weeks before the birth of his first grandchild, Grace Ohana Smith. He had a bulletin board dedicated to her with her ultrasound picture in the middle, her name at the top, and hearts inscribed all around. In his bathroom, after he died, I found a little yellow plastic brush that he'd used for decades to groom his beard. It had once been part of a doll set I had as a little girl. When our son Benjamin Albert Smith was born four years later, we marveled at how he looked exactly like my father. Benny still sticks his tongue out when he's concentrating, just as his grandfather did.

As per his wishes, my sister Chelsea Townsend and I deposited most of his ashes off of the northern California coast into the great Pacific, the first body of water that captured his heart and defined his essence as a man of the sea. We saved the rest of them for Airport Beach in Cedar Key, which was his favorite place to have our regular hukilaus, and where he earned my forever name for him, Pop-the-Dot.

Hope this book makes you proud, Pop-the-Dot. Our time wading, swimming, diving, boating, sampling, eating, and just being together on the ocean left a profound impression on me, and instilled a deep love and sense of protection for this magical planet and her peoples. I miss you and love you forever.

ACKNOWLEDGEMENTS

THANK YOU TO the village of remarkable people I am so fortunate to make this journey with. My incredible family, who supported this project over many months and years in both words and actions: my mother, Deborah Townsend; sister, Chelsea Townsend; husband, Dan Smith; and children, Grace Ohana and Benny Albert. I am so, so lucky to have your love, and hope you know how much I return it! My best friend of over forty years, Emily Huang: We are forever bonded, heart-to-heart, and your unconditional love and support over the decades is part of what gave me the courage to write this book. My Zen teacher, Valerie Forstman Roshi: For years, I did not write out of a sense of "lack," but your guidance, compassion, and encouragement to keep exploring reality, dissolving self-doubt, and discovering authentic purpose has elicited transformation that continues as a lifelong path. The Matheson History Museum in Gainesville (mathesonmuseum.org): for being my very first point of contact for research for this project, and for starting me on a journey of investigation that has seeded a love of learning about our history, including ideas for the next books. Cedar Key Historical Society and Anna Hodges: for very graciously reviewing the historical accuracy of the novel, welcoming me into the CKHS fold, and putting up with me contacting you regularly (www.cedarkeyhistory.org). Rosewood descendants, spokespersons, and storytellers Ebony Pickett and Michele George: You welcomed this project with such graciousness, support, and warmth, and have been so generous with your time, friendship, and resources. Albert Fuller: for a wonderful conversation about the Strong family history. Charlotte Willa Burgess, direct descendant of Polly Emateloye Parker: for reviewing the manuscript for accuracy and representation, and putting up with my many Facebook messages. Dr. Debra King, Professor of Literature, Women's Studies, and African American Studies at the University of Florida: for your counsel on sensitive language usage in the context of this story. Ben, Josh, and Jill at 1842 Grind and Mercantile and Meghan, Elizabeth, and Trevor at 83 West/29 North: two of my favorite Cedar Key eateries that so generously put up with my vegetarian/gluten-free requests and allowed me to sit for hours and write. Dr. Edward Gonzalez-Tennant: for your work on the Cedar Key and Rosewood cemetery sites (www.virtualrosewood.com). Robin Gillies: for offering lodging in your beautiful home so I could have immersive writing time, your beautiful and whimsical artwork (rbngillies@gmail.com), and doing yoga together. Crystal Solana Bryan: for being available and willing to work with me on short notice to share information about your Los Floridanos heritage. Ranger Andrew Gude, Commissioner Jim Wortham, and Lighthouse Keeper Kenny McCain: for updating me on the status of the Seahorse Key bird disappearance. Dr. Leslie Sturmer: for speaking with me about your incredible work bringing clamming to the Cedar Keys (shellfish.ifas.ufl.edu/about-us/leslie-sturmer/). Tiare at Save the Manatee Foundation: for explaining the current threats to manatees in Florida (savethemanatee.org). Nature Coast Biological Station: for answering my various species identification queries (https://ncbs.ifas.ufl.edu/). Captain Bobby: for spending a beautiful afternoon taking my daughter Grace Ohana and me on an educational clamming excursion (https://www.captbobby.com).

Tidewater Tours (www.tidewatertours.com): for wonderful shuttles to Seahorse Key. Marci Lipschultz-Mroz: for critically reviewing the manuscript and making very important edits and suggestions. Editor/Mom Deborah Townsend: for your investment of time and talent in critiquing the manuscript through its various stages and offering invaluable feedback to improve the flow of the story. Line editor Marnie Wiss: for generously offering your valuable time and incredible skills to make sure this novel received the benefit of your exceptional editing. And finally, St. Petersburg Press: for welcoming me into your family with such warmth, shared vision, and support.

CONTENTS

FOREWORD

THIS BOOK IS a fresh body of words that will take you on a journey of HEALING. With a unique twist of events and details, readers will get a sense of history and acknowledge it, and begin to lean in and move forward into moments of peace, hope, and tranquility.

Since the beginning of time, WATER has represented our totality. It cleanses, feeds, relaxes, baptizes, heals, and sustains US! All of US! It connects US! The elements of life encompass the earth and enable us to replenish, release, repent, receive, remain, regain, reaffirm and respect one another. Though the storyline is fictional, the historical events represented in this book are true. Prepare yourself for a riveting and engaging novel where history and nature intersect.

May we forever remember MY FAMILY who loved, lived, survived, and thrived there....Will you take this journey of HEALING with me???

May we forever remember....ROSEWOOD, FLORIDA.

--Ebony Pickett, Evans Rosewood Family Branch
President of Rosewood Family Reunion, Inc.

I know,
You blame me
Because,
If I
Had not been
They
Would not have
Dangled
Your Brother
Your Sister
Your Father
Your Mother
... From my limbs...
Please forgive me
Had I known
If I could
... I would have
Plucked myself
Up
By
The Root!

--Excerpt by E. Stanley Richardson, "Century Oak: A Conversation with a Tree" (1)

CHAPTER ONE
PROLOGUE (1983)

"UM, ANY QUESTIONS?" Jase rocked nervously from one foot to the other, facing a stone-quiet classroom. His classmates stared back, shifting uncomfortably in their seats. *Oh, this isn't good*, thought Jase. *I should have picked something normal, like how my dad helps me improve my basketball shot. This is why we never talk about it. What was I thinking?*

At last, someone's hand slowly went up.

"Isabelle?" the teacher responded eagerly, ready to cut the silence.

"Um, so, Jase," began Isabelle tentatively, "you never actually *met* your great-grandfather?"

"Well, no. He was murdered in 1923, and I was born in 1970, so I never met him." A low murmur went through the seventh-grade classroom. The teacher, while maintaining her composure, revealed a deep crinkle in her forehead.

Another student asked, "So, why did you pick a relative you never met for your report on a family member who influenced your life?"

Jase was measured in his reply. "His story hasn't been told outside of our family yet. We've been keeping it to ourselves for sixty years, 'cause everyone's been so scared, but my daddy said it's high time for everyone to hear it. My grandpa told my daddy, and then my daddy told me, and now I'm telling you."

Their collective tension eased, so Jase continued, "My great-granddaddy Sam Carter died when a mob of white folks believed a lie and burned down his whole town, just about thirty miles west of here in Rosewood."

"What was the lie?" asked Isabelle.

Jase paused before answering. *How do I explain to a bunch of other middle-school kids that a married white woman was having an affair with a white man while her husband was at work at the saw mill in Sumner, and that the man she was seeing beat her, and to cover for herself she said she was assaulted by a black man?* He took a deep breath. "Oh, you know, the kind of lie everyone told back then during the Jim Crow days. We studied it in Civics. A white person did something wrong and blamed it on a black person. Gave the whole community in Sumner a reason to start lynching and burning without even so much as a slap on the wrist by law enforcement or the government, and my great-grandpa Sam was the first one they got. He was lynched, hung from a big live oak tree, a lot like the ones we have right out there in the schoolyard." Everyone's heads turned to follow as he gestured out the window. They gazed solemnly at the statuesque trees for a long moment, seeing them in a whole new and sobering way. Spanish moss hung heavily from extended limbs and swayed gently in the slight afternoon breeze in the same way that good people's limbs once swayed from these same branches. Limbs hanging from limbs.

"My daddy took me there once, to Rosewood," Jase continued, "but it's private property these days, so we can't go back. We don't know if or where my great-grandpa was buried. There's no gravestone, no anything to remember him by 'cept that huge live oak tree. So we've decided that the tree is his resting place now. My daddy told me that great-grandpa Sam and my grandpa Sam Junior loved that big old tree. My grandpa used to climb all over it when he was a kid like us, before the.... massacre."

The students shifted uneasily in response to the word. After a short pause, Jase continued. "He told me that great-grand-pa Sam's grandpa, my great-great-great-granddaddy, came from a place in Senegal, on the west coast of Africa, where trees were considered sacred. We don't have the same kinds of trees here in northwest Florida, but he loved all kinds. So, you know, it just made sense."

"Were there other people murdered?" blurted a boy in the back row. The teacher shot him a look for not raising his hand, but it didn't matter. Jase felt momentum now, emboldened by the questions from his classmates and the support of his lineage.

Jase replied, "Well, yes, at least five others were shot dead for sure. Maybe more. They were all my great-grandpa's friends, too. And a lot of folks got beat up bad, or worse. Some stuff happened that was so bad I can't even talk about it. The rest of the folks from the town escaped and fled all over the state, and some of us direct descendants are still right here in Archer, which is one of the first places folks escaped to. Every time my daddy drives me to go fishing in Cedar Key, we stop at the Rosewood marker and look in at all the trees. We imagine that everyone who got killed is resting there now. We imagine that the land still remembers the happier days before the massacre, when everyone lived, worked, and played together for a few generations in that beautiful place."

"Sounds like Rosewood was once a wonderful community," offered the teacher.

"It was," Jase concurred. "My daddy told me that before January 1, 1923, when the massacre started, it was one of the happiest African American communities anywhere. And that was a really bad time for African Americans, which made

Rosewood all the more special. There were even a few whites living there, in the big house you can still see from the road. Nobody thought anything of it. My daddy thinks it's partly because everyone had a good job at the Sumner mill or in turpentine, and they had really nice churches and a good school and a social hall and a Mason lodge and plenty to eat, but also because everyone lived in the middle of the forest, and nature always takes care of us. Now it's just nature there, taking care of the dead. There's still an old cemetery back in there somewhere, but no one can visit it anymore since it's all on private property. There are no more buildings. They were all torched in less than a week. Nothing but the old Wright house still stands."

Jase concluded, "Great-grandpa Sam's favorite trees were the live oaks and eastern red cedars that grew around Rosewood and Cedar Key, but that one huge live oak right where he lived, worked and was hung from was like part of his own heart, he loved it so much. So he died where he loved to live, and so now we can tell the story. Now it's my turn to tell it, and maybe my telling it will help people treat each other better. Maybe it will help make things better for African Americans and other people too. And that's why my Great-grandpa Sam Carter influenced my life the most."

Feeling a tenderness towards Jase, the teacher asked him, "And did your great-grandfather also pass on his love of trees to you?"

Jase looked out the window as a sudden swift breeze palpitated long strands of sun-illumined Spanish moss draped from the elegant, strong arms of the schoolyard live oaks, and his heart moved.

"Yes," he replied. "Very much."

CHAPTER TWO

THE SPIRIT OF SAM CARTER (2022)

SUNRISE. STEAM RISING from dew-dusted leaves, a gentle ruffle of stirring, warming, summer air, a kiss goodbye from the rising fog, a twitter of creatures through leaves and branches. Oh, to be alive! To be cold sometimes, warm other times, still and calm or thrashing and flailing, to be crawled upon, bored into, fed by sun and soil and water, to feel the current of water rising up and flowing down the breadth of my ever-expanding, en-crusted trunk. To feel roots crawl downward and reach outward through the endless meters, tendrils eagerly connecting with a rich sub-ground biome and caressing the roots of my dear live oak family members, thriving here in this glorious near-coast-al upland. To enjoy the steady sensation of a widening trunk and expanding canopy, gently but firmly reckoning with my neighbors for air and sunspace so that we may all grow together. Harmony. Freedom. Each moment, new and unrepeatable, yet so familiar, so beloved, so sacred. All of this, simply being a live oak tree.

Sometimes animals gather in my shade: Florida panther, bob-cat, raccoon, opossum, armadillo, black snake, green snake, black bear, coyote. They like to pee on me, climb on me, scratch against me, mate, fall asleep, move on. On this dawn, there's a herd of deer next to me, twitching tail and nostrils as they enjoy tender clumps of the sweet grass that thrive in my mottled light and rich soil. This soil, my roots tell me, is among the uncommonly richest of this sandy, ancient maritime bed that we all spring from. I'm one of the biggest trees here, and beneath me is some of the sweetest, greenest wild grass east of the Gulf of Mexico. I'm intrinsically aware that without the sun, soil, breeze, birds, squirrels, grass, mammals, reptiles, insects and all, there would be no me, no heavenly existence that is "tree."

A steadiness in me holds it all. For hundreds of years, I've been right here: hundreds of summers, many hundred times three-hundred-sixty-five sunrises, sunsets, and moon-caressed nights. That moon, always my companion, even when those with eyes can't see it. There is a great blessing in being able to see and hear without eyes or ears. There is simply an is-ness, so that clouds and storms and phases of waxing and waning never obstruct the companionship of my constantly full, bright, moon.

The deer are fidgety today: twitchy and uneasy. They hear something, and their heads rise in quick succession as they forego breakfast in an increasingly alarmed state. This is nothing new, as deer are inherently uneasy, but then I sense something too: large mammal sounds. Not a bear or bobcat, but something much louder and clunkier. Rather than the crack of twigs or rustle of branches, these sounds are like a steady and rising murmur, accompanied by rhythmic footfalls. The murmuring sounds are vaguely familiar, coming in swirling vibrations as if from wisps of memory. The buck in the herd stomps his hoof three times.

A warning.

White tails now fully erect, all of the individual heads in the herd lift from the scrumptious grass in unison. Some still chomping, the deer bound synchronously away, deep into the hammock.

Minutes later, the large mammals gather in my cool early-morning shade, laying out tables with jars and shovels and *speaking to each other softly and somberly. There are about thirty of them, of all different sizes and with different colors of trunks and branches and leaves. Xylem and phloem stir inside of me as one of them, so beautiful with her slightly wrinkled bark, her curly, wiry shock of white canopy, and a trunk the color of rich, dark, organic swamp soil, steps in front of the rest. She makes murmuring vibrations that I somehow understand:*

"Today we gather at this site of a once flourishing African American community that was erased—no...violently eradicated–by racial violence nearly one hundred years ago. We gather now in awareness and remembrance for a soil ceremony to honor those who were terrorized and murdered here. Please bow your heads as we light candles and say their names."

Some of the mammals have water flowing from their eyes. They lower their canopies, and a fresh sadness grows within me, as if my sap is connected to theirs.

"Sarah Carrier. James Carrier. Sylvester Carrier."

Wait, I know those names...

"Lexie Gordon. Mingo Lord God Williams. Samuel Carter."

Samuel Carter. Samuel Carter. Sam Carter. I definitely know Sam Carter.

I tremble so much that leaves rain down upon the gathering. Water pumps faster up my trunk. Sugar encrusts my roots. This "Sam Carter" is intimate to me. My very own bark. How? "Sam Carter" is not the warmth of dawn, nor the scuttle of squirrels, nor the cackling and pecking of pileated woodpeckers, nor the uptake of water that are all me. But I feel "Sam Carter" in my roots and sap and leaves and acorns. His cells and atoms are right here.

Suddenly, my umbilical connection to the moon and sun and breeze is severed. There is a rush of blinding noise: the accusa-

tions, the taunts, the derisive laughter, the gunshots. I smell the smoke and sweat and whiskey, and feel a memory so real that my heart—a human heart—pounds of my trunk in terror. I separate, floating and disembodied, torn painfully from my tree in a sudden recognition

I am Sam Carter.

Me, Sam Carter: carved to pieces under me, this tree, my own blood soaked fully into this soil. My ear and hand must have decomposed somewhere nearby; after my killers carved them off, I oozed and seeped deeply into this ground that spades were now collecting and placing tenderly into labeled jars bearing my and my neighbors' God-given names. My ear, my hand, my blood...must have been mighty fertilizer, concentrated as it was with my humiliation, my fury, my tears, my grief, all held by me and Sarah and James and Lexie and Mingo and Sylvester and our families and generations of our ancestors, all concentrated in our cells and bones and marrow. Of course. Of course. This very tree that I am, this tree is where I once made a living as a blacksmith, taking machine parts that were scattered over the ground and hauling them on ropes over this tree's sturdy branches. On January 1, 1923, it was my own parts scattered on this tear-strewn ground before I was hung over the tree myself: carved up, shot, lynched.

And just like that, I am no longer the tree, nor the scuttle nor the pecking nor the warmth nor the breeze. I am separated from the Heaven that the sunrise and the wind and that moon and I shared for the past one hundred years. Sam Carter, me, now as singular and separate as these mammals.... these....people I am floating over..... Oh dear Lord Almighty, my heart is breaking!

I remember...everything. The jeers. The smell of smoke and moonshine, burning, and old rope. The searing pain, the hot wet salty drippings of my blood and tears. The panicked fear

*for my precious son, my beloved wife, my brother, my niece,
my neighbors. The cold, clear, blue eyes that stared at me, filled
with hate, before the trigger was pulled. The CRACK that was the
last thing my human form heard through its one remaining ear.*

At once, Sam flew—literally—into panic, as he raced wildly about the surrounding tree canopies, calling their names.
"Aaron? Scrappy? Y'all here? Wake up! Wake up! We still in
Rosewood!" He looked down at the gathering of humans,
and then honed in on the speaker. She resembled his long-
time neighbor. "Janie, that you?" But being the first to die,
he couldn't have known that his kind neighbor, Janie, who
always gave everyone a fresh pie each holiday, was brutally
assaulted while her husband was dragged behind a car and
left close to dead before they escaped to Bronson with the
help of the Levy County sheriff, Bob Walker. Sam couldn't
have known that his neighbor lived the rest of her life traumatized and intensely fearful, directing all of the kids in her
household to run-not-walk home from school, to get upstairs
quickly and hide if someone came to the door, and to never
too conspicuous, for any reason, ever.

Janie's daughter, now elderly but once one of the kids who
grew up in that fear-soaked household, stood in somber silence in front of the gathering. She gazed into the eyes of each
attendee with an austere, matriarchal focus, saying without
the need for words, "Remember. And do NOT let history repeat itself."

The resemblance was uncanny, and Sam was confused.
"Janie!" he cried out to the elderly woman. "That you?!"

Only cicadas answered. He saw the deer herd, now safely
ensconced behind the Wright house, the white house, the
only remaining house left in Rosewood, which once belonged
to its only Caucasian residents. The deer were comfortable

now, contentedly chewing that sweet dark grass that tufted in treat-like clumps out of the fertile soil. There were bones and blood and terror in that dirt, growing soul-infused soil that fed the sweet grass that fed the white-tailed deer. When he flew over the grazing deer, they seemed to notice. They lifted their graceful heads and, with grass-stained mandibles still grinding away, perked up their bright white tails and bounded nimbly over to where Aaron Carrier's house used to be. *Aaron Carrier*. His good friend and neighbor. Whisked away by the sympathetic but mostly powerless Sheriff Walker right before they came for Sam. Maybe Aaron was killed in Bronson, or in Gainesville, for all Sam knew, or maybe he made it out alive.

Where are the houses? The churches? The school? Where is everyone I know?

He raced through the swamps of Gulf Hammock and Wylly and then to the old mill site at Sumner where the unspeakable horror of the Rosewood massacre erupted from a single lie. Only a few appendage-like concrete and brick-lay stumps remained, but Sam remembered: A white housewife named Fannie Taylor, beaten by her white lover, started off the frigid morning of the first day of 1923 by shrieking pitifully to her neighbors that a big bad black man had broken into her house in the early dawn hours and attacked her. Some said she even accused this imaginary man of rape. Within days, that single, self-protective lie boiled up violent, mob-fueled expressions of bigotry, fear, and self-declared supremacy out of the motley pot of a self-righteous white community. Fannie's clueless, revengeful husband led the weeklong rampage that followed, turning Rosewood to dust, blood, and bone.

Since Sam had been the first to be lynched, he didn't know what happened after that, or where everybody was. But now, seeing as there was no more hamlet of Rosewood, he imagined it must have been very, very bad. He cried out again, "Wake up! Wake up! Y'all? What the hell happened? Where in the world is everyone?"

If he'd gone about twenty-five miles to the east, he might have found Janie's children, nieces, nephews, and grandchildren living in Bronson. Or, if he'd darted south to Pasco County, he would have found a whole community of descendants whose grandparents fled to Lacoochee to pick up work at the mill there and get as far away from the memory as they could manage. He would have also seen the descendants of Fannie Taylor: she, her husband, and their children all ended up at that same Lacoochee mill when the Sumner mill burned down a couple of years after the pogrom. He could've gone to Tampa, Gainesville, southeast Florida, or any of the other places where a diaspora of Rosewood descendants from the original seven family branches lived. If he had, he would've seen the ones who were passionately devoted to the memory of Rosewood, working to build awareness of what happened, and the ones who, out of shame, fear, guilt, or just old-school recidivist-allegiance to a divisive cause, wanted it to stay on the down-low. And, if he'd only known, he would've seen his own grandson Jase Carter, an associate professor at the University of Central Florida, right below him at the soil ceremony.

But he only knew his beloved home in Rosewood, the mill in Sumner, and his favorite fishing holes a few miles west in the nearby coastal village of Cedar Key. Like most southern communities in his time, the Cedar Key of 1923 was segregated. But just like with Rosewood before the massacre, blacks and whites were generally friendly with one another. African American Cedar Key residents enjoyed a fairly comfortable

living working in the fiber and cedar mills or fishing, attend-
ing community events, and playing sports. Some even held
political office.

Back when he was alive, Sam had a few close cousins there
on the Hill in Cedar Key who loved to fish. When Sam was up-
tight or tired after a long week of blacksmithing, Cedar Key's
soothing waters and natural, peaceful beauty offered refuge.
After Sunday church services, he sometimes went to Cedar
Key to worship at the altar of the tides and marshes. The choir
of seabirds and salty breezes was his gospel, and the sacred
sounds merged with his very essence. It felt a lot like when
he was a tree, and he suddenly wanted that feeling back.

As if in synchrony with his longing, the sticky, humid air
suddenly shifted westerly, and it carried the sweet-salt scent
of the Gulf. Feeling lonely and distraught in his disappeared
Rosewood and having nowhere else to go, he rode the summer
breeze nine miles west to Cedar Key. Just under the whoosh
of the flowing air, a suggestion of a sound flirted with his
remaining ear:

Chhhhooooooooooo—kooooooohh....

He listened harder. Gone. But that one whisper affected
him like a siren song beckoning him to fly faster to his sanctuary by the sea.

What we now call Cedar Key is actually Way Key, the main
inhabited island of the Cedar Keys, an archipelago of islands
situated in the wide crook of Florida's underarm. To Sam, it
looked much the way he remembered it, with little development in a century's time compared to the explosion of stucco
Dollar Generals and sprawling outdoor malls called "village
town centers" across the rest of the state. The concrete pier
had replaced the old wooden one and was four times as big,
and people now dashed around in little golf carts, but folks

still fished peacefully from their jon boats and off the bridges, pulling in sheepshead and trout, casting nets for shad, finger mullet, and glass minnows. The old African American Mount Pilgrim Baptist Church there on the Hill was boarded up. But the Hill was still there, its historic homes now restored and occupied by white folks, reinforced to be safe and dry from climate-change-enhanced rising full-moon tides. And there, looking as half-dead as ever, was that same old knotty tree Sam remembered, its roots cracking through old asphalt.

Sam's outspoken, pre-civil-rights activist cousin Floyd had mysteriously disappeared from the Hill one summer in 1921. Rumor long had it that he was lynched here at this very tree, then thrown to the sharks before anyone could point a finger. Rumor or real, it was a warning: black folks, be happy. Ain't nothin' wrong with the way things are, so don't talk out of turn. Looking around now, seeing no more black or brown folks living on the Hill, Sam couldn't help but remember that too many former residents, his kin, weren't always as content-ed as they were supposed to be. He used to think to himself: if only they could live like we do in Rosewood, thriving inside and out, doing things as we please. And yet, they had good times together, him and his cousins, in Cedar Key. They fished hard and ate well and were friendly with everyone in the town, black and white alike.

He called out to his closest extended kin: "Cousin Floyd? Man, you here? Wake up! It's me, Sam!"

He listened, waited. Sparrows fluttered in and out of the nests tucked inside the hardened, peeling branches of the salt-worn tree, and chicks opened their beaks to feed. A pungent sea breeze carried the vegetable smell of low tide and set the crackled, dry leaves to rustling. A sad and tiny cedar tree, a lonely remnant of the once-vibrant population of trees the archipelago was named for, kept crooked company.

Sam was still desperately alone. But then...

Chhhhoooooooooo—kooooooohh.... There it was again, coming directly from the Gulf, from the direction of nearby Atsena Odie Key.

A magnet was set to him. Sam darted down historic 2nd Street to A Street until it curved around to Dock Street, and then, testing his new powers, he dove into the Gulf of Mexico. He hovered mid-depth in the water and listened again, through the clicks and clacks of marine life and distant hums of outboards, but heard nothing to assuage his loneliness and confusion. Instead, his mind was left with busy, troubled memories that came through as frequently and randomly as the endless underwater chatter. The memories that came up most fiercely were the many stories of folks from the lynch mobs saving small parts of their victims in jars, and then throwing the rest of each cut-up body into the Gulf like common chum. For the first time, he noticed that his watch was gone from his wrist, above the stump where his hand used to be. In a panic, he glided erratically through the pilings around the pier, looking for bones, skulls, trinkets, his watch, anything. But he only found striped hermit crabs riffling over barnacle-encrusted plastic bottles, tangles of fishing line and hooks, six-pack rings, beer cans, and cigarette butts, and his heart became so heavy that he settled with it into the deep murky bottom of the boat channel. "This ain't right," he muttered, submerged in salty anguish. For lack of phantom tears of his own, the Gulf provided. "This ain't right." He sat there into the late afternoon, and then on through sundown, a time when he and his kin once, around mid-century, would not have been wise to remain and enjoy one of the things Cedar Key is most famous for: its spectacularly colorful Gulf sunsets.

As the pre-moonrise dusk made the murky water even darker, he felt certain that he was not only completely alone but also utterly invisible. He was so overtaken with grief that he didn't notice the striped hermit crabs migrating away from the pier pilings to tap on his one hand and both feet consolingly, checking to see if he might need a fresh shell. He wasn't aware that a pod of curious dolphins had spotted him, clicking the alarm to nearby pods and circling him with concern.

That century oak in Rosewood was smaller the day Sam Carter's limbs dangled like heavy moss from its apologetic and grieving arms. Those same arms gave life back to Sam, inviting him into the real, unconditional wonder of being alive in a way that was far more expansive than he ever thought possible when he inhabited his human form. At sunrise one hundred years later, Sam's spirit, his death, his life, and the life of that tree had been inseparable, and Sam had known that Oneness was his–and everyone's–birthright. At sundown that same day, Sam sank deep into the underwater boat channel muck off of the Cedar Key municipal pier–and even deeper into his bereavement–and felt that everything was all separated and divided up again.

Nearby along the waterfront on Dock Street, a brown-skinned Indian family from Gainesville was getting served more slowly than other customers at a particular seafood restaurant whose owner also owned the Scratch Bar. Later that night in the same place, a tired and thirsty fisherman with broad lips and wiry hair raised a muscled, chocolate-colored arm for a beer, but was ignored for a good long while.

The moon rose far above, patiently seeking her companion.

Thinstripe Hermit Crabs
• •

The thinstripe hermit crab (*Clibanarius vittatus*) can be a wonderful saltwater aquarium pet–for a while, anyway. They are ridiculously easy to catch (unless you don't have a collector's permit, in which case you would likely be the one getting caught). They like to scuttle all over the sandy or oystery shallows, and when you do the stingray shuffle, you're bound to gently knock one over with your gliding toes. If you're collecting for aquarium purposes, make sure you take at least two, and add some empty shells of varying sizes and shapes to the aquarium landscape. Despite their name, hermit crabs are sociable beings and like to tap on each other's shells now and again. Sometimes they negotiate for a shell trade, feeling out the echoes of their taps to see just how much space their friend is working with, to see if they might be better off switching houses. They enjoy trying on different shells every once in a while; exploring their potential wardrobe of empty shell outfits is an enjoyable pastime. They love to eat and check in on each other, and you can even train them to recognize feeding time by a few taps on the aquarium glass. They seem to like other types of crabs too; plop a small *Menippe mercenaria* stone crab in the tank with them and after a few days, once the new crab has carved out a nice little hidey-hole for himself between a couple of well-placed barnacled rocks, the hermits seem to enjoy circling around his little cave entrance and tapping his rock in acknowledgment.

Thinstripe hermit crabs are usually content in an aquarium, for a short time. But no matter how well you feed them, how large their tank is, or how friendly their roommates might be, do keep in mind: Any being taken from the wild, open expanse of its home will fail to thrive once it's boxed in for too long. At some point, it needs to return to the wild, to the capacious potential of its birthright, without borders.

CHAPTER THREE

ISLAND BOYS (1983)

ROY BAMFORD III met Jase Carter, great-grandson of Sam Carter, one day while riding his bike near the Number Four bridge. It was a scorching summer between sixth and seventh grades, and he'd pedaled out further towards the mainland than his pa allowed. But he had heard about the Civil War battlefield just across the Number Four channel, which someone told him he could see from the fishing dock right near the bridge. Besides, he was twelve now, and anyway, he was just going to take a quick peek and not go to the part of the bridge where the black folk fished, which would've made his pa pull out the belt on him if he found out. But when Roy saw a kid about his age pulling up the biggest redfish he'd ever seen, he forgot about all that and went to check it out.

"Dude! Epic catch!" were the first three words out of Roy's mouth. The kid beamed back at him in acknowledgement. Roy asked, "What did you use for bait?"

"Shrimp, plus my daddy's special secret," replied the kid, an answer that acted like its own kind of bait for Roy.

"C'mon, man, ya gotta tell me," Roy begged. "Please—what's the secret?"

The kid was resolute. "My daddy would kill me if I told you."

"Well, can I fish with you some, then? You don't have to tell me nothin'. I'm Roy, by the way," Roy added, extending a fist.

"Sure, help yourself," replied the kid, bumping the out-stretched fist with his own. "My name is Jase." He motioned for Roy to pick up a pole. Roy surveyed the collection of long homemade bamboo fishing poles quizzically, taking in their various lengths and thicknesses, then reached with relief for a more familiar Zebco click reel.

The two boys spent the better part of four hours just fishing and talking in the midafternoon heat. By the end of the afternoon, Roy had acquired a face full of freckles and found a friend—a good friend—easy to laugh, funny as hell, good at fishing, eager for adventure—and now he knew how he wanted to spend his summer. Thankfully, Jase agreed.

On the hottest summer days, Jase and Roy would hang out at Helen's, the candy-striped diner on Dock Street owned and operated by the former mayor, Helen Johannesen. They spent hours playing *Space Invaders* and drinking frothy vanilla and chocolate milkshakes, waiting for the tide to change. Then, they would go running barefoot down the street to the pier, taking turns throwing their cast nets. Captain Throckmorton, the weathered sentry on the old wooden pier, pointed to where the bait were running, and the boys followed his lead, filling bucket after bucket with shad and glass minnows and then bagging them six at a time to sell to the bait shop across the street. There was never a shortage of bait from those fertile estuarine waters, and never a shortage of milkshake money. Sometimes they even made enough for a burger and fries.

The boys would bike over to Helen's every morning, buy a milkshake, and start the endless adventures inherent in island living: bait catching, bait selling, fish catching, bug catching, sand-gnat swatting, swimming, biking, kayaking, snorkeling, eating, laughing, building sandcastles, walking the mudflats for sand dollars, playing basketball at the city park.

One day, Jase brought a small aquarium net to their daily meeting spot at Helen's, and held it up for Roy to see as he approached on his bike. Roy snickered. "What in the hay-ell do you 'spect to do with THAT puny net?" His pointedly eyed the six-foot cast net hanging off of his bike handlebars, as if to indicate "no contest."

Jase snickered back: "Follow me. Watch and learn."

They rode their bikes the short distance to the floating docks at the city boat ramp. Jase dropped his bike, grabbed the net and a glass jar from his backpack, ran over to the edge of the dock, flattened himself on his belly, and hung over the side.

"What the--?" Roy exclaimed, approaching him. But just before he could finish his sentence, Jase pulled up the net, and it was filled with clear jelly. "Great, good job Jase, you caught sea snot---WHOA!" As Jase poured the gelatinous glob into the jar, the snot turned into a wonderland of glass eels, tiny jellyfish, ctenophores, amphipods, isopods, miniscule little shrimp, and a pinky-nail-sized argonaut with a papery shell. Roy's eyes widened. "How? What are all these things?"

"Cool, huh?" Jase grinned. "My daddy showed me this when I was little. We got some aquariums at home, and we were scraping our nets along the dock to try to catch some baby shrimp and crabs to feed our fish, and all this stuff came up. I didn't know what half of these things were, but I went to a marine biology camp last summer and I learned 'em all. But that's not all...." He bent back over the side of the dock and pulled up two brown blobs. "Look closely, Roy. Come up real close and look."

Now fully engaged, Roy put his face right up next to the brown things, waiting to see something else amazing. Instead, he got shot point blank in the eyes and mouth with two surprisingly forceful jets of salt water. "You son-of-a-sea cow!" Roy exclaimed, spitting out the water and rubbing his salt-stung eyes. What IS that thing?"

"Scientists call 'em tunicates, but we call 'em sea squirts! And I got you!"

"Oh, that's IT," exclaimed Roy, who bent over, saw the surprisingly large number of sea squirts attached in clumps next to the oysters along the bottom of the dock, and pulled out a squirter of his own. "Watch out!" Two long streams of water shot out of two nipple-like siphons right at Jase, and the boys started in an ages-old water gun battle invented long before plastic toys. "Hey, wait, what? How do you reload?" Roy's "gun" had stopped squirting.

"Well, they only have so much water," Jase replied. "If you keep squeezing it, you'll kill it. Better put it back." The boys threw the desiccated tunicates back into the water, and Jase carefully poured the glasslike plankton out of the jar as well. Roy was infatuated with this whole new world of sea life that had been hidden in the brown-green water right under his nose all this time.

"Jase, what camp did you go to?" Roy asked, hungry to go too.

"It's part of my school in Archer," Jase replied. "But this summer, my dad has some work out here in Cedar Key, so he wanted us all to stay close to home since no one could drive me into camp every day. So we can make our own camp, you and me!"

School. Roy never considered where Jase went to school. His own school was right there in Cedar Key but so far he'd only learned about cells and zygotes and the layers of the earth in science, not anything about tuna-kates and argonauts. "You all drive to Archer during the school year?"

"Yea. My daddy and momma both work at the University in Gainesville. They drop me off on the way in, every day. But they like living' here, on the water, and we get to be here on weekends and vacations and stuff. So we can still hang out when it's not summer."

Roy didn't understand. He asked, "What, can't they find jobs closer to Cedar Key? Like Otter Creek or Chiefland or something? You know, there are a lot of restaurants and places. I'm gonna apply to be a dishwasher at Salty's when I turn fourteen, bring in some money to help my Ma out. I could ask if you want, see if there are any jobs for them closer to here."

Jase laughed. "It's hard to find college professor jobs anywhere around here but Gainesville, man. University of Florida, you know? Go Gators! One of the top-ranking public universities in the whole country! You can bet I'm going there. Gonna get my Ph.D., just like my parents. And with their Ph.D.'s, I'm not thinking my momma and daddy are interested in waiting tables like they did when they were in college. "

Roy was taken aback. He hadn't even considered that the kinds of jobs Jase's parents had could possibly be anything other than cook, dishwasher, or janitor. I mean, Jase did mention they were at the university, but Roy figured they were in food service or custodial or something. At the tender age of twelve, he checked his conditioning for the first time. And it wouldn't be the last.

Roy and Jase spent the rest of that perfect summer, and the two summers that followed, in the same way: meet at Helen's, have a shake, run out to the pier and hang with Captain Throckmorton, throw their cast nets and catch bait, sell the bait, make more milkshake and burger money, repeat. In the afternoons, they would explore different parts of the island, sometimes wading out into the water, doing the stingray shuffle, communing with the eight hundred or so dolphins that lived in the Cedar Keys. They would bring masks and snorkels and swim through schools of finger mullet and shad, marveling as the fish parted and joined in flashing, silvery, shifting clouds. On low-tide days, they would walk barefoot all the way out to the boat channel, squishing their toes in the muddy sand, digging up quahogs and finding sand dollars and sea stars.

Roy also saw Jase during Thanksgivings, Christmases, and spring breaks. He had a lot of friends at school, but only Jase seemed to be unaffected by all the weird bullshit happening lately, especially as they were turning thirteen and fourteen and some were hitting puberty at lightning speed. With Jase, he didn't have to worry about talking cool, hiding his acne, or acting like he didn't care about nothin', when really he cared about a lot of things and wanted to talk about them. The older he and his friends got, the more some of them started to sound like his pa, talking about people with other skin colors and sexual identities in ways that made Roy really uncomfortable. Roy instinctively kept Jase a secret from his pa, even though each night when he got home, he longed to tell his parents about their many adventures. Ma liked Jase well enough, thankfully, but he didn't dare bring his best friend over when his pa was home. Roy started to think he had to keep his time with Jase a secret from his other friends now too, even though for the past two years, no one had seemed to care. Heck, sometimes his other friends even joined them out on the dock or the sandbar or their adventures. But everyone was changing now.

Even though Roy and Jase were both on the verge of manhood, when they hung out they could still be kids, seeped in the wonders of exploration and new discoveries, fully experiencing the insanely bountiful world surrounding them. One particularly memorable November day, wading way out in the backwaters, they heard a forceful exhale and a splash. They both screamed as a huge body rolled, displaying a rotund belly right in front of them. While Roy kept screaming, Jase started to laugh. Roy, still terrified, asked him: "What are you laughin' for, man? It's a goddamn sea monster! He's gonna eat us! Get outta the water, for god's sakes!"

"It's a manatee, man, relax," said Jase reassuringly. "We saw tons of 'em in Crystal River. He's just sayin' hi, probably on his way over there now, or maybe to Manatee Springs, now that the weather's coolin' off. And the only thing he's gonna eat is your palm salad, man. He's vegetarian."

Roy was saucer-eyed, watching the gentle giant carefully. "You mean....SHE!"

Jase let out a joyful sound as a smaller manatee–though still the size of a pony–emerged beside the larger one. "We-ell, helloooo, momma!" said Jase. "Happy Thanksgiving!" As if on cue, the momma lifted her head as she crunched her plentiful feast of juicy seagrasses in the shallows and gazed at them curiously through her tiny bead-like eyes.

That evening, after they had watched the mother and baby amble away in the golden hour of late afternoon, they lingered at that secret spot on a little sandspit on the backwaters, surrounded by mangroves and marsh grass. The tide was flowing out, revealing copious oyster beds that looked like little dark bumpy islands all around them. They stayed there for hours, as they often did, not saying a word as the dynamic light of day gave way to a different painting every night. Fat mullet pierced the water's surface with scattered leaps of joy at another day well spent. White egrets swooped across the vista, finding their roosts for the night. On this particular evening, the sky was cosmically purple, with a few darts of orange slicing like the fingers of the sun, waving good night.

Roy and Jase both felt thankful. Their world was whole, and good, and abundant, and they had each other to share it with.

That was the last time they saw each other for almost forty years.

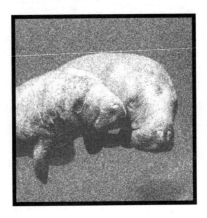

Manatees
••

Of all of Florida's most iconic animals–alligators, pelicans, panthers, dolphins, flamingos, and more–there is none quite so beloved as the West Indian Manatee. A marine mammal comparable in size to a small whale, manatees can reach lengths of up to fourteen feet and weigh upwards of 3,000 pounds. They are Florida natives in the truest sense, with their own Florida subspecies: *Trichechus manatus latirostris*. They have lived in Florida for 45 million years.

Despite their prehistoric origins, however, there is some evidence that manatees may actually be smarter than humans. Studies of manatee brains have revealed that while they don't have as many crenulations, or folds, as human brains do, they have a much higher ratio of gray matter to white matter. Their apparent intelligence is especially interesting when considered in conjunction with manatees' most notable characteristic: they are entirely peaceful in disposition. Snorkelers and scientists alike have marveled at how manatees show affection for their immediate family members and express distress and grief at the loss of another manatee. Many will even gladly accept belly rubs from humans. Unfortunately, it is precisely their gentle, easy-going nature combined with their preference for shallower waters where their favorite seagrasses grow that makes them especially vulnerable to injury or death from outboard motors on fast-moving boats.

Manatees eat between fifty and two hundred pounds of seagrasses and aquatic weeds per day, depending on their size, taking seven or more hours to leisurely consume ten to fifteen percent of their body weight's worth of food. When they aren't grazing, they spend the rest of their day sleeping, playing, relaxing, exploring, and caring for one another. This may be the best evidence of all that manatees may very well be more intelligent than humans.

CHAPTER FOUR

ROY THE THIRD (2022)

GROWN-UP ROY BAMFORD the Third didn't have a leg
to stand on. He lost it during Desert Storm, to an exploding
underground mine that jettisoned him high in the air and
right into a huge rock face that cleaved off and crushed his
femur into tiny bits. He'd baked in the sun for hours, dazed to
near unconsciousness, blood seeping like a little creek from
his body into the sand, wondering why in the hell his boys
weren't on it, treating his wounds and getting him to the med-
ic back at their encampment. His boys would have been on
the job for sure, if they hadn't been scattered in parts in the
sand all around him. Days later, in and out of surgery and
blood transfusions, lying in a medical gurney on a plane back
to the States, he found out that he was the only one in his unit
who had survived.

His family had been fishermen in Cedar Key for three gen-
He went home to Cedar Key after his honorable discharge,
which included a brief ceremony, a gunshot salute that almost
made his head explode with equal parts pain and terror, a little
medal, and an ID card that would grant him free medical care
at the VA hospital in Gainesville for the rest of his goddam
life. That was it. Leg gone, friends gone, soul gone and nerves
shot to hell, and they expected him to just go back to fishin'.
Bastards.

His family had been fishermen in Cedar Key for three generations. His granddaddy had come down to the Gulf with
visions of Opportunity dancing in his eyes. He worked for

the cedar industry and invested in David Levy Yulee's new Florida Railroad before railroads were even a glint in the more famous Henry Flagler's eyes. Cedar Key was to be the hub of the South, with its prolific rose-colored cedar pencil industry, fiber factories, and busy railway system steaming into Florida's fertile future of environmental exploitation and profit. Enterprising young Roy Bamford I invested his family's life savings into the sure thing and waited for the money to start rolling in. If not for the damn hurricane that wiped out the pencil mill and most of the cedar trees in 1896, it might've been a lucrative investment. Roy III, now without a leg to stand on, might have been baron of a very wealthy family had Mother Nature not so rudely and violently intervened.

Stranded, penniless, and desperate, Roy I took what he could from and joined the burgeoning net and longline fishing industries. Quite unlike the posh, well-heeled vision of his cedar pencil and railway business dreams, his days became long and hard. Sometimes he fished for grouper, sometimes flounder, sometimes sharks, sometimes oysters, and he had specific rigs, nets, lines and traps for all of them. He traded in his dapper business clothes for denim overalls, muck boots and sun caps, his briefcase and fancy contract-signing pens for poles and nets and oyster rakes, and eventually earned enough to buy a sturdy bird dog. Since people still had to eat and he now had a decent rig to get out to better fishing grounds, he was one of the few to maintain a steady income during the Great Depression. But convinced that the pencil industry would have survived the crash, he stoked the fires of his own Great Internal Depression, holding fast to the conviction that he woulda coulda been a millionaire with a fancy plantation house and a dozen black servants if the Almighty hadn't forsaken him, that he was cursed by Satan for God-knows-what reason. He took out his rage on his wife, his son, and anyone he could lord over, including the then-thriving and very free African American residents of Cedar Key. He connected with the official Ku Klux Klan chapter in Gainesville and became a self-proclaimed Grand Wizard of his own unofficial Cedar Key chapter. Once a praying Protestant, Roy the First lost all his faith and died an old, angry, and curmudgeonly man, but not before he passed it all on–fishing skills, depression, alcoholism, racism, and atheism alike–to Roy Junior. Roy Junior's quiet, faithful, and seriously abused ma, codependently unable to exist without her devil of a husband, died two weeks later in her bed.

Roy the Second started drinking and smoking in high school to stave off the back pain and sunburn endured during his long hours out on the Gulf pulling net and longline hauls. He married his high school sweetheart when she became pregnant, dropping out during their senior year so he could fish full time to support his new family. From age 17 on, his days were exactly the same: get up well before dawn, fill up his coffee thermos, fill up his rum canteen, point his bird dog to whatever fishing ground was running, fish all day, come home at sunset, unload and process his haul, eat dinner with the annoying wife and their bratty kid Roy the Third, have a beer, complain (on good days) or yell and hit (on bad ones), collapse into bed for a few restless hours, and repeat. Roy the Second's anger and abuse extended well beyond the walls of his home, as he was infamously known for instigating failed lynchings all over Levy County as the (usually inebriated) new Grand Wizard of the county's secret, but pretty much official, self-declared Ku Klux Klan chapter. He often spoke proudly of the KKK mob that took the time to travel all the way from Gainesville to "take care of them n— in Rosewood,

and it's my job to make sure they never forget, just like my Pa."
His drunken declarations sounded surreal and insignificant to
young Roy the Third–who was busy being a barefoot island
kid living in paradise with his best friend–until the dark day
that the ramblings came home to their own living room.

It was at the end of one of those perfect island childhood
days with Jase that Roy the Third came home to find his Ma
crying because his pa had just been arrested, again, this time
for beating up an African American man who was a ten-
ured university professor and lived just east of the Number
Four bridge. The man was on the island looking for his son,
Jase, when Roy the Second approached and laid into him in
a drunken fury, first with his fists and then with a nearby
razor-sharp oyster clump, threatening him with a lynching
if he didn't "keep to the mainland." The battered man was in
the hospital in Gainesville, Roy's bitter, drunken pa was in
jail, and Roy, heartbroken, felt the mortification his pa had
always inspired in him turn to steely hate.

Roy the Third didn't see Jase for the rest of his childhood.
Each day during the remainder of that Thanksgiving break,
and then on Christmas and spring breaks and into the following summer, he'd rode his bike all over, and as far east as
he was allowed to go without crossing the bridge. But Jase
never came, never even fished on the other side of the bridge,
and still harbored his daddy's secret way of catching monster
redfish. *And why would he?* Roy stewed, churning with disdain, embarrassment, and remorse about his pa's inexcusable
actions.

Roy spent the rest of that last summer hanging out at Hel-
en's, looking up expectantly when the door jingled open. But
only pink-faced tourists and leathery fishermen rotated in
and out of the red-and-white-striped oasis. Sometimes, he'd

fiddle for quarters from his dwindling stash of bait money and play grief-stricken songs on Helen's jukebox, especially Genesis's: *There Must Be Some Misunderstanding.*

One morning, the always-smiling, always-sociable Ms. Helen served a dejected Roy his milkshake and asked, "Where's your friend been all this time, child?" She couldn't help but notice that young, sad, Roy had already played Genesis three times that morning, with a splash of Tom Petty's "Don't Come Around Here No More" and a hit of Aerosmith's "Hole in My Soul" thrown in for good dramatic measure.

"Dunno," was all Roy could muster with downcast eyes. Helen's smile faded for a moment, but then returned along with a consolation offer: free milkshakes for the rest of the summer. Roy accepted with a weak smile, appreciating her compassion, but it hardly compensated for his sense of powerlessness, or the fact that neither he nor Helen could bring Jase back in through that door. For the first time since those first few quickly forgotten moments when he and Jase first met, he thought about Jase being black and him being white and how that had somehow screwed up the best relationship he had ever had. It was totally unfair, and his pa sucked.

When Roy the Third got big enough, he defended his passive, defeated mother from his father's physical abuse with ever-increasing physical strength and resentment. But the yelling and drunken fury kept up until Roy the Second died at age 39, probably from a combination of liver failure, lung and skin cancers, an ulcer, high blood pressure, a heart attack, depression, and maybe even suicide. Since his only doctor and only medicine had been a rum bottle, no one really knew for sure. They found him adrift on his boat, with a blacktip shark gaffed and equally dead beside him. They buried him and the shark together in the old Cemetery Point Park next to his father and mother, with a small headstone that read simply, "R.I.P. Roy Bamford II, son of Mary and Roy Bamford I." Last time Roy III had checked, all three graves were covered in detritus from the spring tides, which got so high these days that even the lines of quahog shells cemented in careful rows over the tops of their graves wouldn't keep their bones from completely submerging and dissolving permanently into the murky matrix of the Gulf, and someday soon.

His mother seemed to get happier in the years following her abusive husband's early departure, though she'd never admit it. It was almost as if she still feared him, believing he could rise from six feet under and wallop her upside the head if she gave him cause. She held a steady job at Cedar Key High School as an administrative assistant, told people's fortunes as a side hustle for grocery money, and life was stable and quiet until Roy the Third went off to bring shock and awe to America's enemies.

Now Roy the Third–the last in his line–stood on his remaining leg on his family's crumbling old dock, staring at the bird dog resentfully. *Damn dock can't even moor the boat anymore, it needs so many repairs,* he thought, realizing with irritation that he was going to have to trailer the bird dog to the city boat ramp till he could make enough money to repair the dilapidated dock's planks and pilings. And then what? Catch what? Since those bountiful pre-war days of every kind of fishing imaginable, the state had cracked down hard: the fishing was impacting the fish and the oystering was impacting the oysters and the crabbing was impacting the blue crabs and stone crabs, whattaya know. And by "impacting," the scientists meant that overharvesting was leading to their disappearance from these waters. Gill netting was banned, bag limits were imposed, crabbing was severely regulated and oystering was

prohibited, all in the early nineties while he was bleeding out
in the desert. Scientists from the University of Florida and the
Fish and Wildlife Commission started coming out in droves,
collecting, tagging, lecturing, imposing. Roy had come home
enough of a hot mess as it was, but losing his one possible
livelihood—fishing—was a devastating blow. He resented the
scientists, those clean-cut city-lookin' folks from places with
official names like Institute of Food and Agricultural Sciences
(IFAS) and Harbor Branch Oceanographic Institute (HBOI).
They seemed to think they knew these waters better than
he did just from reading all their books and getting degrees
and giving lectures. They just showed up, hardly sunbaked or
calloused at all and prone to seasickness at any sign of chop,
and felt like they had the right to tell him what to do.

But Roy changed his mind about some of the scientists
when Dr. Lisa Storm came along and suggested a whole new
maritime industry: clamming. Admittedly, it wasn't as dynamic and adventurous as offshore fishing, but it was a way
to make a living out on the water that he could adapt to well
enough. Dr. Storm was a true outdoorswoman—not book-
ish like the other university-types he'd met—and she led the
charge to create vast tracts of clam "farms" out by Dog Island
and other areas around the twenty or so keys that opened into
the Gulf of Mexico. Turns out, the nutrient-dense waters, with
their regular flushing by fresh water from the open Gulf, were
about the best clam environment anywhere, and now Cedar
Key, once famous for its cedar tree and fiber products and
swimming-type seafood, was becoming known as "Clamalot."
Dr. Storm even offered training and leased out tracts of underwater land—two acres per plot—at a price he could actually
afford with the help of her hard won state-funded grants.

He found himself considering the oyster beds exposed in

front of him with the falling tide. Dr. Storm and her team tried to farm oysters here, too, same way they tried up in Apalachicola, but the oystermen were still too unwilling to let go of wild oystering to accept farming. There were a few oyster farms, though, even though raising oysters was a lot more work than raising clams. The Apalach oystermen, desperate to uphold their reputation as the oyster capital of the world, would try to sneak into Cedar Key waters from the Panhandle to "steal" what they could, but the Cedar Key oystermen detected them and set their boats on fire. They held fast to the old ways until they just couldn't anymore—first the oysters became contaminated with salmonella from runoff from faulty septic systems in the Suwannee, and then, after all that mess was fixed, there just weren't enough oysters left to support the industry. But you'd never know it now, gazing out during the low tide. Roy marveled at how big and clean and healthy the oyster beds looked right in front of him. Still, it was clamming that was the future of Cedar Key. And, he realized grudgingly, he was gonna have to figure out how to keep doin' it for the long haul.

Dolphins cracked the surface of the water and interrupted his brooding—an unusually large pod even for these rich waters. They seemed determined to capture his attention. His heart skipped with joy for a wisp of a moment, but he was so mired in his physical and mental pain that he quickly regressed into pensiveness. He was keenly aware of the place where the uneven nub of his upper thigh rubbed uncomfortably against his ill-fitting standard military-issue prosthetic, and just as keenly aware that it would be a living hell to clam like this, convinced more than ever that the Bamford family was indeed cursed.

He hadn't even been able to hold onto a steady relationship.

He'd returned from the war looking heroic, handsome and buff. His missing leg seemed to be some kind of a war hero turn-on to the single ladies in town and even a few discerning men, and there was no shortage of interest. His first girlfriend post-war was a stunning blonde who doted on him, especially when they were out in public. He couldn't help but notice, however, that she winced with revulsion almost every time he unstrapped his prosthetic leg before they made love, revealing a contorted and uneven red scar and a flaccid flap of skin where his knee used to be. Still, their relationship lasted for a good six years, long enough for him to build up the courage to buy a ring and try to figure out how to get down on one knee when he only had one knee. The night before he planned to propose, he found out that all through the last three years, all the times when she told him she was working late or visiting relatives in Bronson, she had been sleeping with another man who happened to have two fully functional legs.

Since then, Roy's relationships had been short-lived and dysfunctional. Over the past ten years he had preferred to just avoid the insanity of dating altogether. Sometimes, though, he felt a longing to love someone genuinely with the small part of his heart still left unguarded–the part that could still strike a joyful beat at the sight of dolphins.

At least Ma was all right these days, happy to have him home and alive and almost in one piece. She cried less often than she used to, too, and these days her tears seemed to flow more out of relief than anything else. Roy the Third maintained a deep love and protectiveness for his Ma, and that gave him a reason to give clamming a go after all. He would make his Ma proud. He would break the dysfunctional patterns of his family and break the Bamford curse. He would be the Grand Wizard of the Ku Klux CLAM.

He noticed the pod of dolphins again. They were always there when he was on the water, keeping him company, always smiling, gratefully ready to receive any chum and fish guts he could spare. He cracked a dolphin-like grin. For just a moment, despite years of growing pessimism, he felt an odd grounding, a sense of meaning to everything that was faintly familiar to him, as if programmed somewhere deep in the matrix of his cells. It happened other times too, like when he knew he had to help his Ma, or when he noticed the sparkles of light on the backs of the gathering pool of dolphins coming towards him from the direction of Atsena Odie. It happened a few times when he felt a warm love for his army brothers, or when he started to feel something more deeply for a girl that had nothing to do with how good-looking she was. Sometimes it sprang up during a particularly remarkable sunset, or when a magnificent frigate bird sailed regally overhead. Sometimes it arrived with a sound that came in on a gentle breeze from Atsena Odie–*Choooooo-kooooohhh*–that made him tingle with a sense of innocent play. It reminded him of those carefree days he spent as an island kid, with his best buddy Jase, just free and fun and easy.

A part of him wanted to understand that odd but familiar feeling, but it always dissolved before he could wrap his mind around it and reel it in. And then, sure as day, whenever it seemed his heart could finally understand and might point the way to some sense of happiness, his mother cried inconsolably, his unit brothers died, his girlfriend cheated on him, the sun set, the frigate bird got caught up in a fishing line and drowned, the gentle breeze turned into a Category 4 hurricane, his best friend was gone forever. Even the ever-smiling dolphins seemed uneasy these days.

Bone-dust through my fingers. What good's a peaceful,

easy feeling when it just leaves me high and dry every time?
My grave's gonna wash away too, in our crumbling, ill-fated
family plot. Grandpa was right. The Bamfords are cursed.

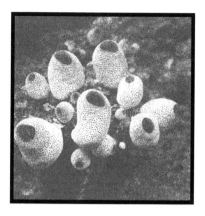

Tunicates
••

At first glance, it's hard to believe that the larger singular tunicates, called ascidians, are even alive. In fact, they are actually in the phylum Chordata, which means they are more closely related to vertebrates like us than to invertebrates like clams. Tunicates come in a vast array of types–a combination of colonial and singular, sessile and mobile varieties–and in a whole palette of colors. Clues about their close relationship to vertebrates appear in their larval stage, when they resemble tadpoles and feature a nerve cord that runs down their backs. They spend only a few hours in this stage, likely using their nervous system to hone in on the most ideal spot to settle in and attach their heads, where they'll live for the rest of their remaining lifespan of approximately one- to several-years. When transitioning to their sessile form, they also form their signature leatherlike outer covering, called a tunic, which is made up of cellulose and is equally protective and pliant. Recently, scientists have discovered that the tunic contains anticancer properties and can also be used to help repair or even grow damaged human tissues.

Marine and medical researchers have also long been fascinated with the bidirectional pulmonary system of tunicates.
They have a built-in pacemaker system that seems to work
better than our own, making them ideal models for learning
how to treat heart issues in mammals.

Once they have settled in on a suitable oyster clump, dock
piling, or rock, tunicates' nerve cords are reabsorbed and they
develop into their adult form, well-suited to a life of taking
water in through one siphon and expelling it through another,
enjoying a constant, omnivorous buffet of plankton.

A tunicate lives a life of relative stillness, adapting to and
thriving with the dynamic ebb and flow of the tides.

Chapter Five

EMATELOYE (2022)

WHILE SAM WAS sinking—literally—deep into the muck and Roy the Third was backing his bird dog down a boat ramp full of tunicates, a marine biologist named Emma Tiger Burgess stood thigh-deep in the water collecting echinoderm specimens from the fertile seagrass beds just off the shoreline of Seahorse Key, three miles down the main boat channel. Emma tried to focus on her work, carefully raking through clumps of seagrass for sea stars, but waves of heartbreak kept pulling her out with the waning tide. She blinked her eyes, fighting upwellings of tears. As they finally broke, a breeze curled through the sticky air, waving the reaches of *Spartina alterniflora* marsh grass so dramatically that their tips folded over with the weight of the *Littorina* snails tossed about. And then...

Chooooooooooooooooo.....

"Yes, Great-Great-Grandmother, I know..."

Koooooooooooooooooo.....

Home. Come Home. This beach, the breeze, her broken heart. Home was everything just as it was, if she could just let it be so. She heeded the familiar guidance and gave up her attempts to squelch her tears. She released them, her heart, all her grief small and large, until their salts merged with the Gulf in a stream of just one tenderness.

Perhaps it was the way that the seaweed piled up in neatly scalloped lines during the falling tide on the shores of

Seahorse Key that made her look closer. All those little shrimp and crabs and barnacles flailing for oxygen.... She wanted to grab the chunks of detritus and throw them back into the ocean, knowing full well that there was nothing she could really do about this ancient cycle of rising and falling, highs and lows, life and death. Rather, it was the unjust, unnatural, unnecessary suffering that she could rise to, just like the tide would rise over and over again with the whole of the planet to gently bring the still-living, growing beings home while the expired and blackening seagrasses and animals baked into the sand.

She gazed out over the choppy channel between her and Way Key—better known as the main island of Cedar Key–the only key in this archipelago attached to the peninsular mainland by a narrow umbilical ribbon of two-laned road. She drifted into memory. Her research had brought her from her south Florida home in the swamps of the Big Cypress Seminole Indian Reservation to the shores of the Gulf of Mexico, first to Tampa Bay's Egmont Key and now to this one-hundred-sixty-five-acre island. The two sites shared a very dark history in her people's past. How ironic, she thought, that she was committed to working now to save the people here, after so many of her own people suffered and died in these places. But that was the way she had been taught. "Getting back" at people who wronged you, stole your land, killed and imprisoned your ancestors, and who treated you with poorly concealed prejudice was not the way of her people. To achieve harmony, she was taught and believed, one must live in harmony.

Despite knowing these things, her heart was tender at this time. She was still reeling from a breakup with a man who had been enthralled by her Native American looks but unable to see past them to her exceptionally gifted brain, her eco-warrior spirit, and her extraordinarily generous heart. When the novelty of her faded– after one exhilarating, exhausting, intimate year– in favor of his sudden infatuation with a fluttery-eyed and much younger exchange student from Japan, she began to question whether she'd ever be able to have a meaningful relationship. After all, this scenario had become a chronic pattern: she meets someone, they fall hard for her, charm her, win her, get distracted by the next novelty, and leave. She was done with it. She was crushed by it.

Men were assholes.

She let her thoughts and worries spiral outward, away from her great-great-grandmother's grounding advice through the ethers, away from home, away from the wonder of this present moment. Her tears almost obscured the sight of breaking fins, splashing tails, and the clear plea from the dolphins:

Chooooooooooooooooo.......Koooooooooooooooooooooooo!

Emma wasn't entirely sure when she had first known that her great-great- grandmother, Emateloye "Polly" Parker, was watching over her. Well, not "watching over" in a worldly sense, as Polly Parker had long since merged with the ancestors, but somehow for Emma, Emateloye still lived outside of time as a sort of guiding reality. It sometimes felt to Emma like it was the only true reality, one that existed everywhere and nowhere, and was linked directly to Emma's soul, heart, body, and mind. She recalled a time when she was six: she and a swamp-sized rattlesnake caught each other by surprise in Big Cypress. The rattler coiled into a flat-headed strike position as she recoiled in response. She remembered how terrified she was, her heartbeat escalating in concert with her raw fear and the increasing fervor of the snake's sizzling tail. And then, a sudden breeze fluttered between and around them, drawing down her heartbeat in perfect synchronicity with the lowering head and abating rattle of the mollified viper. She heard a feminine whisper: "Chooo-koh." It was the Maskoki word for "home," but she knew, somehow, what it meant beyond words and definitions. She walked left, while the snake slid right. Her fear was whisked away in the breeze, replaced by mad respect and a calm, abiding knowing beyond her six short years.

When she went home and told her parents, her mother smiled and looked through the low ceiling of the small kitchen of their double-wide. "Oh, great-grandmother," she said, "Emateloye has your name for a reason. Thank you." And that's when Emma knew that Emateloye Estenletkvte, her great-great-grandmother and her namesake, was the great Polly Parker, and that Polly Parker was with her always.

And Polly Parker was great indeed. During the infamous relocation efforts by General-then-Governor-then President Andrew Jackson to imprison and relocate Florida's native Seminoles—by then a proud hybrid tribe of native Potano, Timucuan and Miccosukee descendants, southeastern Creek, various other tribes, and runaway African American slaves who had escaped to Florida–three ferocious Seminole Wars took place. While United States forces successfully captured many Tribal members and transported them up Florida's west coast and the Mississippi River to join the Trail of Tears, others eluded capture. Still others, like Emateloye, used more creative means to make sure that the Seminole Nation became the one Unconquered Tribe.

During the Second Seminole War, Jackson's soldiers captured Polly Parker along with her husband Chai, and forced them to help the government track and capture other Seminoles. The couple led the soldiers in circles, at ease with the copious gators, moccasins, and redbugs in the swamps of south Florida, purposely finding no traces of fellow tribal members in the slippery Everglades. True to their loyalties, they "tracked" through conditions so sticky, hot, wet, and buggy that the unacclimated white men were repeatedly unsuccessful at rounding up many Seminoles under Polly and Chai's "guidance." Jackson's inhumane efforts were relentless, however, and over three thousand Seminoles were ultimately captured and relocated to Oklahoma. With the death of the great Chief Osceola, even with no formal treaty or declaration, the Second Seminole War was over.

For about fifteen years after that war ended, life fell into a short, uncomfortable peace, with only about three hundred Seminoles remaining on their native Florida lands. Despite their loyalty, Polly and Chai were treated like outcasts in their own tribe, since many of their brethren were unaware that their "tracking" had been intentionally ineffective. But in 1855, the government began eyeing what remained of their land, Chief Billy Bowlegs took up arms, and the Third and final Seminole War exploded. U.S. soldiers recruited Polly and Chai quite against their will to scout again, but this time they openly objected. A gunshot found its way through Chai's heart; legend says that it was Polly herself who killed him, rather than releasing him to once again scout for an army intent on eradicating those who remained of her people. Polly was captured along with Chief Billy Bowlegs and one hundred sixty-one other Seminoles. They were imprisoned in horrible conditions on Egmont Key at the mouth of Tampa Bay for a time, and then loaded onto a boat called the Grey Cloud. Cramped aboard the clunky steamer, they chugged for twenty-two hours up the Gulf. They steamed past the Cedar Keys, past the old Seminole internment camp at Seahorse, past Atsena Odie, and up to the Florida Panhandle, where the boat finally moored for refueling. It was only meant to stop for a few short hours, before continuing on to the Mississippi River on a route that has come to be known as "The Voyage of Tears." Polly, Billy Bowlegs, and their kin were all bound for reservations in Oklahoma.... That is, if they survived the trip.

Many of the Seminoles on board were very ill. Most of them had already suffered weeks of malnourishment in rancid, unsanitary conditions in an internment camp on Egmont Key, much like the one located on Seahorse Key just up the coast during the Second Seminole War. Polly, trained in herbal medicine, persuaded her captors to allow her and twelve assistants to debark to search for herbs for medicine, convincing them it would make the rest of the trip easier. A guard was dispatched with them, but he could not come close to matching Polly's mastery of the wilderness. She and her fellow Seminoles quickly disappeared into the forest, using animal sounds to reconvene after losing the guard. Though the soldiers rounded up six of the escapees when the alarm was sounded, Polly and the remaining party of six continued to travel swiftly, mostly by night, in harmony with the alligators, snakes, and mosquitoes. Polly led the group a full four hundred miles back to Fisheating Creek on Lake Okeechobee, the heartland of the Unconquered Florida Seminole Tribe, in only four days.

And there is where Polly's phenomenal story became legend. She remarried and had a daughter, Lucy Tiger, who had a daughter, who had seven children, who had seventeen children among them. The Seminole Tribe grew and grew, and today many Seminoles can directly trace their lineage back to Ma Emateloye, including the tribal chairman, a medicine woman, the tribal president, the governor's adviser, the director of casinos and gaming in Brighton, the director and curator of the Ah-Tha-Thi-Ki museum, the janitor and the P.E. teacher at Ahfachkee elementary school, and a marine biologist currently thigh-deep in the water off of Seahorse Key, collecting sea stars.

Emma didn't know if others of her shared lineage were cosmically connected to Polly Parker, but for her, it was unquestionable. Sometimes, Ma Emateloye came to Emma through the breeze, and other times through the rustle of leaves, the rhythm of her breath, or the rush of flowing water. This afternoon, when the breeze and the water couldn't break through Emma's trance of heartache, Polly Parker sent the dolphins to relay a very, very important message.

Emma relaxed her shoulders, re-grounded her feet, and listened deeply. She focused on the dolphins and slowed her inhales and exhales. And then, there it was: that universal communication that speaks only through the melding of heart, mind, and breath.

Your heartache: we know this. All beings know this. Today you are crying with another. You are both part of the cries of the whole world. This other one is right here, right down below us here, and his heart is broken so completely that he has forgotten that he is part of us and part of you. Do you hear him? He is not alive. He is not dead. He is an ancestor who is lost. His voice is sinking into the mud beneath us now. He sounds so alone, but he doesn't know we hear him, just like we hear you. Perhaps now you can hear each other, and you can cry together and go home, to that place before and after death. Before and after sadness. Before and after we came to believe we were all separate from each other. Before and after we forgot we are the same Source. Go to him! Go!

Emma blinked as the dolphins submerged. All those years

of feeling the subtle energies of the snakes, the birds, the breezes and blessings around her had made her deeply aware of interconnection, but this? Did the dolphins just communicate directly with her using words? Perhaps the cracks in her heart invited a deeper opening, and she allowed tears to flow even more freely now, in sobs that were cleansing and clarifying. She sent a message through her tears and into the Gulf:

Sir, please hear me. Let us cry together. You are not alone. I will do all I can to ease your pain.

Somehow, she knew that whoever was underneath the water was also underneath her own smallness, and that she would devote herself to listening ever more deeply for the voice that could invite them both Home.

Bottlenose Dolphins

Over eight hundred individual bottlenose dolphins (*Tursiops truncatus*) live in the waters around the Cedar Keys. Despite the fact that they cannot endure much fresh water, the estuarine richness of the Suwannee's outflow merged with the eastern Gulf provides one of the most reliable and nourishing food courts any marine mammal could ever wish for. Conditions are so spectacular for dolphin wellness that Cedar Keys *Tursiops* have evolved a particular style of fish-hunting unique to their superpod: they assign roles, with some dolphins "driving" the fish-of-choice, while others line up and form a "barrier," like a living net. The result is a fish haul to rival that of the most experienced seiner. This team-tasking is so advanced that the dolphins of this area have achieved considerable fame in the marine science world.

When not hunting, the dolphins of the Cedar Keys spend equal portions of their days socializing, resting, and traveling around an area of about forty square kilometers. They vocalize vociferously, inviting studies into the nature of their communication. With brains larger than those of the arguably more ego-driven *Homo sapiens*, and lives that appear to be generally content and free from human-like drama, it is very possible that dolphins have advanced brain abilities that humans can only aspire to achieve.

Chapter 6

THE COLOR OF BONES (2022)

EMMA'S FREELY FLOWING tears, laden with the ancient salts of human compassion, were carried out with the tide. They swirled like effervescent eddies down the boat channel that connected Seahorse and Way Keys, shining like the stars of Van Gogh's famous painting, and finding their way to Sam Carter and caressing his face with the tenderness of a grandmother. He felt his heart shift in a way that released him from his trance of despair. He suddenly noticed the hermit crabs, the approving dolphins, the gentle waft of current against his ethereal skin as the spring tide flowed. It was the closest he'd felt to what he'd known during his century as a tree since the separation happened.

He began to move, to look around, to examine his surroundings with a fresh sense of purpose. The word "home" sprung forth into his consciousness. He emerged from the mud and looked around. Something light and long caught his eye and drew him like a magnet. He picked it up and at once recognized four of his own fingers, attached to his own palm, all bone and no skin now but still somehow known and missed. He looked at the stump of his wrist thoughtfully. Except for his ear and his hand, the rest of him was still attached. How did part of him end up deep in the mud of the boat channel?

If he'd even considered such a heinous possibility, he could have spirited himself over to the Scratch Bar on Highway 24, where dusty glass jars lined shelves on one wall near the ceiling. The bar was chronically dim and smoky, and most of the jars were too old and crusted over to see what was inside; but if you looked closely, you could catch a hint of a shark's fin, a bird egg, a snake, a human finger. And when someone there would ask what time it was, the hundred-year tradition had become to answer: "Well, lemme check old Sam Carter's watch."

But of course, this possibility didn't occur to Sam, and he was simply grateful to have most of his hand back. Against the dark and algal mud of the channel, it looked so very, well, bone colored. *All that hate and horror,* Sam mused somberly, *all for the color of my skin. We all got the same-colored bones.* And with that one clear thought, he floated his corporeal form right out of the water, carrying his non-corporeal hand bones with him.

At that moment, Emma felt a rush of cool air on her tear-stained, smiling cheeks. She didn't know Sam, but she'd learned from Polly Parker to trust the forces expressing themselves all around her. She understood that, at least at this moment, both she and the other being crying nearby felt a little less small and a little bit closer to big, and she relaxed. He would be all right, and she could return to her work. It was time to bring her samples back to the Seahorse Key marine lab.

Sam felt a lot better, but unlike Emma, he didn't know what he was going to do next. Getting more accustomed to being a spirit instead of a tree or a human and remembering the ineffective state of panic he formerly succumbed to, he chose a different tactic this time: to hover, listen, and wait. Suspended between the low clouds under the full moon and the glassy surface of the water, he let himself be lulled by the sounds around him: wavelets lapping on the quiet shore of the small public beach at the city park, oysters sputtering little spurts of water and clicks of air as they closed up in the lowering tide, lovers ardently kissing on the rock jetty, fishing lines zipping in and out from the municipal pier, a slightly out-of-tune guitar accompanying the singing of "Cheeseburger in Paradise" on a nearby bar deck. He breathed in deeply, and much to his surprise, discovered that his senses were alive, as alive as if he were alive, and he relished the unique and familiar blend of Cedar Key aromas: salt and seaweed and outboard motor oil and fried hush puppies and smoked mullet spread and fish guts and coffee and beer all in one satisfying olfactory morsel. For the first time since the separation, he enjoyed a few minutes of hearing, smelling, seeing, and feeling content with things just as they were on a midsummer Thursday night in the heart of Florida's second oldest town. Just like when he was alive, when he could find a place to drift on his boat in solitude on the quiet backwaters, out of sight from any people who might remind him directly or indirectly of how unwhite he was, he found peace and sanctuary. It was the closest he had ever come to knowing Jesus outside of the Good Book.

Jesus. The very thought of his savior Christ and the Almighty Lord God made his heart expand, but it was only temporary. Once his mind began to activate, his heart closed self-protectively, and he began to ponder: *If the good Lord could give me all of this beauty, this peace, these senses, my wife, my son, my heavenly life as a tree, then why has the Lord forsaken me with equal amounts of horror, torture, prejudice, murder, separation and now...whatever I am now? Wasn't I a good man, Lord? Didn't I fulfill every expectation you had of a loving and grateful son? I went to church every Sunday, and sometimes on Wednesday. I treated others kindly. I prayed and sang with so much fervor and gratitude that my heart sometimes felt about*

to burst. I didn't cause trouble, no trouble at all, even when I
sometimes just wanted to be like Sylvester Carrier and make good
trouble when the Sumner mill white folks treated us so badly.
But I kept my head down, an' I still got killed and killed bad, and
now this. Why, Lord God in Heaven, why am I in Hell? And why
do I still feel your presence, your LOVE, in this condition? Please,
Jesus, dear Lord, Holy Spirit, help me to understand.

He closed his eyes tightly and held his one hand and two
wrists to his chest in prayer. Eddies of wind danced around
him—midsummer wind—the kind that is so moist and warm
it can't cool you down. He felt the wind, the warmth, the wet-
ness, and then suddenly, everything went cold. He shivered
down to the spectral version of his singly colored bones, felt
the wind shift and chill, and then heard the wails.

Sam may have been a spirit, but the wails made him shudder. Even if time and space were unclear for him, he at least
knew he was of right mind and in this world; these sounds
were insane and otherworldly. And sad. They were so sad.
Despite his fear, he rose higher into the air and caught the
cold current that carried him towards the rising, clamoring
grief. It was the only thing he could do, the only indication of
what his next step would be.

He drifted over the hill and along the shore, into the
backwaters, and up a low berm to the Cedar Key cemetery.
He passed the well-marked graves with the layers of ero-
sion-quelling quahogs, the honored military heroes and the
generations of well-known white families of Cedar Key, and
found himself over high ground on the far side of the cemetery. There was only one gravestone there, marked "Adeline
Tape, 1858-1927." Around that one stone, there was a stand of
tall pines, a few small and salt-weary live oaks, some weathered cedars, and piles of chaos.

Streaks of angry, terrified, grieving spirits raced around the gravestone and him. "Hello?" he attempted, but they were unreachable. He thought he could make out images of people he might have once known—maybe a cousin, maybe a former resident of the once-bustling African American community in Cedar Key. But they would form and dissolve so quickly in peals and shrieks, and their faces were so distorted, that he couldn't quite tell for sure.

He realized: these souls had never been laid to rest. Rather than the carefully manicured graves down by the ever-rising water and up on the high hill of the cemetery, curated with flowers and trimmed of weeds along the borders, these folks came to Adeline's resting place—the one black person who somehow got a headstone—and waited. The more years they waited, the more destitute they became. Until they are laid to rest, Sam reasoned, they are imprisoned here. And it's driving them mad.

Now this, he recognized, THIS is Hell, and an undeserved one. Somehow, when he was murdered, his own drifting soul was embraced by the grand Century Oak that he'd worked under for so many years. And since his death until now he had only known Tree. Even without a proper memorial service and a gravestone, he had somehow escaped this hellish purgatory. Despite his current disembodied state, his one hundred years of unconditional being sustained him, kept him clear of mind and compassionate towards the uncountable unaccounted deceased swirling around him. His heart ached for them. He tried harder to reach them.

"Friends! Cousins! It's me, Sam Carter! Of Rosewood! Remember? We fished together! We worshiped together! Surely somebody can remember?"

The ululations escalated. They were deafening. His words

only seemed to draw out deeper desperation and new levels of torment. Perhaps, thought Sam, it's too late. Perhaps their grief has consumed them. Is this what will happen to me, too, now that I'm separated? He felt fresh pangs of despair, but he resisted them—they were the siren songs that would take him down a dangerous path. There had to be another way. He sat down to think on a small blank slab of cement that was probably a baby's grave.

"Ssssam? Sammmmmmmmm!" a voice began in a twirling whirl all around his ear. "Sammmmm...Sammmmm...Carterrr-rrrr...." And very slowly, a form appeared in front of him. It was his cousin Floyd. "Sammmmm! Heeeeeelp uuuuuuuuusssss. We got noooooowhere to goooooo. Aaaaaalla Cedar Keeeeey and Rosewoooooood is heeeeere but weeeee done give uuuuuup. We give uuuuuup. Heeeeeeellllp, Saaaaaaam!" His voice and form wavered.

"Floyd! Wait! Rosewood is here too? Why here? Why? We had our own cemetery!"

"The graaaaaaaveyard been grooooooooown ooooooover, been traaaaaaashed. Weeeee beeeeeeeeen looocked ouuuut. Noooooo oooooooone could come paaaaaaaay respects. Nooooooo moooooore resting plaaaaaace for any of uuuuuus. We found each other heeeeere, at Miss Aaadeeeeelliiiiiine's toooooooomb, but noooooow we stuuuuuuuuuuuuuck. Wheeeeeeere you beeeeeeeen?"

"I don't know, Floyd," Sam replied, "but I've been OK. Now I gotta figure out how to help us all. I gotta get us home."

"Howwwwwwww?"

"I don't know," he responded, "but I'm gonna figure it out, my brother." The elixir of Emma's tears, carrying the vital power of Emateloye's invitation home, stirred within him.

Quahogs
....

When one thinks of Cedar Key clams these days, a small, golden, and delicate bivalve comes to mind, about two inches across, agape in a plate of garlic butter at any local seafood restaurant. To fully understand the historical importance of clams and other bivalves to the Cedar Keys area, however, one need only drive a short distance from Way Key down County Road 326 to the Cedar Key Shell Mound, which is part of the Lower Suwannee National Refuge adjacent to the Cedar Keys National Refuge. Here exists the largest ancient Native American midden on the central Florida Gulf Coast, an ancient site for sacred burials, summer solstice celebrations, and feasting, and large enough to create a twenty-eight-foot-high hiking trail composed entirely of oyster and clam shells. It seems that Cedar Key bivalves have been feeding Gulf Coast inhabitants for a very long time.

There are two main species of clams found in the area. The one on your dinner plate is almost certainly the smaller *Mercenaria mercenaria*, also known as the northern quahog, which supports an important aquaculture industry. This northern quahog is not native to the Gulf but was brought over as broodstock from its natural digs in the Indian River Lagoon in east Florida, specifically for aquaculture purposes. There is also a much bigger, thicker-shelled species called *Mercenaria campechiensis*, or the southern quahog, which is native to western Florida Gulf waters. While not as desirable for eating, these clams have historically given their shells for a host of utilitarian uses, from making food bowls to stabilizing buildings and graves against changing weather, tides, and climate change.

Speaking of climate change, scientists are currently working to improve thermal tolerance of the hard clam through genetic selection to produce a clam that is more resistant to the longer, hotter summers and increasingly warm Gulf water temperatures. For the industry to remain sustainable on an ever-unsustainable planet, we must adapt and find ways to support environmentally sensitive practices that do not harm the ecology.

Chapter 7
CLOUDS (2022)

THE TIDE WAS low. Roy was feeling a bit excited, because low tide is a good time to fish, and he hadn't been fishing in a long time what with clamming being his main job these days. Oh, he always had a few lines out, brought home a trout or redfish for him and Ma. But it wasn't real fishing like he and his pa used to do, way offshore where the Suwannee's outflow can't reach and the Gulf turns blue, before all the net bans, bag limits, and other regulations. One day a few months ago, he happened to see a small ad in the Cedar Key Beacon asking for fishermen to help with local research for the Nature Coast Biological Station. Turns out they were starting a new marine pathology study, related to sea-level rise and changing water chemistry or salinity or runoff or something like that. Seems like that's all the scientists around here ever talked about these days. For this study, they needed experienced fishermen to catch, tag, photograph, and release sharks, and then upload the data to their site. Just thinking about shark fishing gave him a little jolt in his core. It was probably the most exciting kind of fishing there was. He answered the ad, got the job, and while the money wasn't quite as hot and regular as it was with clamming, it sure was fun. He needed some fun.

Underneath the brown murky waters of the Cedar Keys swim a vibrant assortment of sharks, some of which are very large for such shallow waters. They thrive in these islands where the warm temperatures and ample rainfall provide

abundant nutrients, freshly streamed in from the overfilling
Suwannee River, for a proper shark egg nursery. The nursery is refreshed daily with the influx of fresh, clean, saltwater from the open Gulf, keeping the otherwise still and
quiet waters well oxygenated. Roy had learned a number of
shark-catching techniques from older fishermen, but he resisted the trauma (to both shark and fisherman) of longlining
and strike netting in favor of the traditional buoy-and-hook
method his old mentor Captain Throckmorton had taught
him many years prior. Over the years, as much as he loved
shark fishing, Roy had turned down a surprisingly large number of offers from underground restaurant suppliers to supply
shark fins, a practice that had always been immoral and was
now illegal to boot. He didn't care about catching sharks to
eat, but chopping off their fins and dumping them back in
the water just seemed cruel, and an insult to one of God's
perfect creations.

Low tide. He could head out towards Seahorse now without
getting grounded, set buoys and hook lines on the changing
tide, do a run to his leased clam farm tracts out by Dog Island to check on the health of his penny seed starter bags,
then coast back to check the hooks when the water was high.
There was a full-moon spring tide too, the best for fishing, the
worst for getting grounded on the oyster bars and sand flats
when the tide begins to shift. Fortunately for Roy, he knew
where all the shoals were, and if for some reason he wasn't
sure, he could read the clues in the ripples at the surface of
the water like a steely-eyed tracker.

The odor of low tide was thick and musky as he readied his
boat at the city ramp. It was the same boat ramp where Jase
had shown him the magical world of plankton so many years
before, and occasionally, when the tide smell was particular-

ly pungent, that day came back to him, eliciting equal parts gratitude and biting sadness. He imagined the secret world of crystalline, gelatinous glass eels and ctenophores just as Jase had revealed to him, pulsating iridescence beneath the slightly oily sheen of the tannin-infused water and the bustle of burly seamen and their shiny black Mercury outboard engines. He looked down wistfully at the tunicates, exposed at low tide, clamped up tightly like the oysters to conserve water. He wondered how many boaters never realize that these two-valved wonders, these sea squirts, were anything more than brown blobs. He got caught spellbound for a moment, as he sometimes did, until the rev of the next truck ready to launch a boat knocked him back into task-mode.

It was the way that his tribe, the tribe of alpha guys, communicated with each other. Revvv...REEVVVVV.... By the time the engines gun on full decibels, the rule is ya gotta either defer or challenge. Roy would have loved to have lingered just a bit longer by the ramp before heading out for a long, hot, day of fishing: To breathe in the floating aromas of bacon, coffee, and outboard motor oil, to admire how the glint of morning sun creating shiny geometric patterns on the ripples of the water, to read the patterns in the sunrise clouds. But he didn't feel like challenging the grizzled, blue-eyed, beefier-than-him guy with a set of plastic testicles swinging from the hitch at the lower rear of his big red truck.

Roy exhaled, gave a quick wave to appease the man in the testicle-adorned truck, and jumped into action. He got his skiff launched and tethered, ran back up to his much-smaller gray truck, sloshed it off the ramp and into one of the many trailer-long parking stalls bordering the launch area and the city beach park. The boat was already fully equipped with buoys, polypropylene line, poles, bait, gaffs, rakes and hand nets for a hybrid day of shark fishing and clamming, so all that remained was to grab his personal provisions from the truck–hat, sunscreen, pork rinds, and four gallons of drinking water–and head out.

When he returned to his boat, he heard the faint rumble of thunder to the east. It was too early in the day for thunder. The weather patterns didn't make sense to him anymore. It had always been the law of land and sea in the summertime: that heat rises all morning and brings thunderstorms in the afternoon. But things were wonky lately. The scientists would say "climate change." Some of the locals would say they were full of fear-mongering bullshit, but Roy couldn't deny that things were different. He made a mental note to stay within three miles of shore, in sight of land, just in case one of the ever-more frequent and occasionally very severe no-name storms materialized.

Despite the potential weather, it was a gorgeous morning to be on the water. The channel was glassy and smooth, the air moist and sweet. A fleet of frigate birds sailed majestically overhead, bound for Snake Key. The dolphins took to his wake almost immediately. There were so many of them lately! He pointed the skiff to the Main Ship Channel, an unusual S-shaped throughway that kept bigger boats from grounding as long as they didn't try any cute shortcuts. Sunrise was particularly pretty this morning, with an accumulation of distant clouds to the east casting a pastel glow. He noticed a peculiar northeasterly breeze coming in, a further sign that weather was definitely coming in early. He'd have to work quickly. His first stop would be the waters between Seahorse and Snake Keys, where the biggest populations of sharks hung out. He opened up the throttle and followed the channel three miles towards Seahorse.

Roy was accustomed to spotting at least a couple of familiar folks from his boat whenever he came up on Seahorse
Key: the ranger Andrew, or the lighthouse keeper Kenny,
or any number of University of Florida students collecting
samples or throwing cast nets or just hanging out in front
of the old marine lab. But as he circumnavigated the island
and approached North West Cove, he was surprised to see
someone he didn't recognize knee-deep out in the water. That
would be unusual enough, but this someone–a woman about
his age or a little younger, he figured–was plumb gorgeous. He
slowed down and maneuvered in for a closer look.

Roy had never seen anyone as exotically beautiful. Her skin
was the color of coffee with cream, her hair long and black
with a few shimmering stripes of silver-gray, her arms strong,
her legs long. She was the very essence of what weary sailors
of yore must have fantasized about when approaching South
Pacific islands in the days of Captain Cook. She was clearly
at ease in the water, not at all like the rigid, serious scientists
and awkward students carefully and methodically trying to
handle their sampling equipment and collection gear. She
seemed to just belong, like she had always been there. He was
entranced. His mind went blank. The sound of thunder was
stronger now, but he forgot about fishing, clamming, and the
weather. He felt a surge of long-embedded biochemicals release into his system, course through his cells and overpower
his rational mind. *Uh, oh,* he realized, *I'm in trouble.*

A primordial, hormone-induced urge took him over quite
against his better judgment, and he watched himself revert to
lizard-brained behaviors he hadn't attempted since his more
virile, and far more witless, younger days. He suddenly felt
immensely proud of his physique that was still impressively
toned and taut thanks to long days of hauling clam bags and

pulling lines. He whistled, hooted, and waved, inflated his chest, and started moving things around his boat to show off his broad shoulders and powerful arm muscles. If only he had pounded his chest, he would have resembled a medium-sized albino ape with a bright and somewhat puffy red neck that was not unlike the dewlap of a mate-seeking male anole or the glaring, swollen buttocks of a hamadryas baboon. His gaze remained fixed on her the whole time, earnestly hoping for a response. But she kept her head down, combing the seagrass beds, deep in concentration.

She must not have heard him, he decided. He let his boat drift closer, whistling again, clunking equipment around his boat and flexing every arm muscle he could activate. She was within easy conversational distance now. He shouted out: "Hey gorgeous lady! New around here? Looking for a guide? Looking for me?" He revved the engine enticingly. And it worked! She looked up.

Her deep, black, cat-shaped eyes connected with his. Oh lord, she was pretty. He was almost drowning in the sudden surge of love hormones. She stood upright. He smiled with a full, white, set of decent teeth, relieved that he went to the dentist regularly, unlike so many of his less hygienic peers who sported tobacco-stained pearly yellows. He waved. She lifted her hand in response and then retracted four of her fingers, leaving the one in the middle prominently raised. Roy deflated. She turned away from him and glided back towards shore, taunting him with the curves of her backside, tossing her head back one more time to look at him with the universal expression of utter disgust that roughly translated as: Fuck. You.

What in the hell was I thinking? thought Roy in a state of embarrassment and lucidity. *I see the perfect woman, and I act like an animal. She didn't deserve that. Jesus Roy, you know better. You suck. You ain't worthy of her.*

A sudden northeasterly gust and a slow and much louder rumble of thunder jolted him the rest of the way out of his biochemical bath so that his mind could focus. *Shit, time's a-wasting. I gotta lay these buoys now or never.* He shook off his sense of self-deprecation. *Get back to the channel between Seahorse and Snake Keys. Cut the bait. Bait the hooks. Drop the buoys. Get to the clamming tracts.* He looked to the east and saw pretty but foreboding cumulus clouds, already licking at him with flickers of an unsettled breeze. He figured he had about two hours, max. If he timed it right, he could make it back to the shark buoys from the clamming tracts in ninety minutes and then shelter at Seahorse till the storm blew over.

And maybe then he'd see her again, whoever she was, and he'd do better this time.

Bull Sharks
•••

Few animals induce the almost-Pavlovian sense of terror in the water as much that sharks do. The movie *Jaws* made great whites infamous and, along the way, pretty much sullied the reputation of sharks in general. What most folks don't realize is that the majority of shark species are not aggressive, from the gentle nurse, angel, leopard and whale sharks to a whole assortment of flat sharks. Even the fierce-looking blacktips, hammerheads, and reef sharks will leave you alone unless you are bleeding and/or wearing something shiny that they might mistake for the silver back of a tasty fish.

All that being said, there are three main species world-wide legitimately considered to be unpredictably aggressive toward humans: the great white shark, the tiger shark, and the bull shark. Of these three, the bull shark (*Carcharhinus leucas*) is common in the Cedar Keys and other estuaries along the Florida Gulf coast. And while the great white is the most feared in popular culture, some scientists actually consider the bull shark to be the most dangerous. There are several

reasons for this dubious ranking. First, they have a pugna-
cious personality and a stocky, muscular body that suggests
the shark is hankering to start a fight. Second, they have a
bite that is twice as strong as a great white's. Third, they can
adapt to many different water conditions, able to survive and
thrive even in low- or no-salinity waters, and they will eat
literally anything.

Despite these ominous characteristics, however, bull shark
attacks on humans are extremely uncommon, probably because they don't like the taste of us. However, because people
both like to eat their meat and are afraid of them, overfish-
ing of bull sharks, combined with environmental pollution,
is quickly bringing these sharks close to threatened status.
Though we don't tend to gravitate towards animals that might
kill us, it's also important to acknowledge that bull sharks
are a critical part of the food web that keeps the ocean and
estuaries balanced and life-giving. For humans, living within
this balance means that extensive open water swimming in
bull shark habitats, especially when the water is murky, is
not advised. Swimmers can remain safe for shallower, limited
dips in the Gulf by not wearing shiny swimwear and jewelry,
not swimming in the middle of large schools of baitfish at
dusk, not eating in the water or being near chum or bait in
the water, and always swimming with a buddy.

Chapter 8
BALANCE (2022)

EMMA GATHERED UP her buckets and nets and carried them to the other side of North West Cove, where she had a tiny outboard tied off to a gnarly oak with a trunk that curled low enough to the sand to serve as a nice tether. She surveyed her catch: ten healthy *Echinaster* sea stars, three with lesions; twelve healthy *Luidia* sea stars, four with lesions; and five *Lytechinus* sea urchins, one with a large growth on its mouth parts. It was concerning. Back in 2015, around the time all of the birds mysteriously abandoned Seahorse Key without apparent cause, Emma found her first cancerous sea star. She had been studying the increase in tumors and lesions in these usually resilient invertebrates ever since, wondering if there could be a connection with the exodus of birds. Seahorse Key was the farthest out into the Gulf of all the islands in the archipelago, which explained the past vibrance, health, and diversity of its bird populations, not to mention the abundance of healthy echinoderms that many of the shorebirds feasted on. The gradual decrease in their food's health might have explained why the birds disappeared, except that the birds didn't leave Seahorse gradually. According to the lighthouse keeper Kenny McCain, a sixth-generation Cedar Keys resident of Scotch-Irish descent, he'd gone to sleep on April 19, 2015. When he woke up the next morning, the birds were just gone. He radioed the Nature Coast Biological Station in distress: "Guys, we have some kinda problem." To this day, though locals and scientists alike have their theories, no one has yet come up with a definitive explanation as to why the birds bolted, some even leaving eggs in nests to perish.

It must be related somehow, Emma pondered, watching the healthy and diseased sea stars and urchins ambulate around and over each other with their hundreds of mesmerizing little tube feet. She grabbed one more sample—a simple jar of seawater—and loaded everything up in her boat. Off in the distance, she could see Roy setting his hooks and buoys, and she rolled her eyes. If there was anything she wouldn't tolerate anymore, it was the good ole boys and their coarse come-ons. This guy had been one of the worst, coming in so close and making such a scene that he rippled the surface and then the bottom of her collection area, stirring up the sediment and killing her visibility, cutting her sampling time short. *Asshole.*

Emma hopped on her boat and navigated it slowly around the tip of Gardiners' Point, then aimed for Ibis Point, noting, soberly, that there were no more ibis there. As she eased into the marine lab's dock in Seahorse Harbor, she was comforted to see little spiky feathered heads peeking out of the grand osprey nest, which rested like an artisan's basket at the apex of one of the old lookout poles sticking out of the water. The nest had been freshly built by two newcomer ospreys that spring, much to everyone's delight. There had been a few other new avian arrivals this year too: some egrets, and a couple of great blue herons, presumably from other parts, no doubt wondering how they scored such a beautiful island all to themselves. Only seven years ago, those newcomers would've thought twice about setting up shop in such a crowded habitat. But the once chronic, sometimes deafening sounds of *wok wok wok* and *kakakakaaaaa*, not to mention the tendency for island visitors to receive gloppy bright white "blessings" from the many nesting birds all over the island, were just a memory now. When the osprey whistled, when the egrets croaked, they sounded lonely.

She docked, waved to the ranger and some university students hanging out by the outdoor touch tanks, and started unloading her samples. The old marine lab was right near the dock. Having long passed its mid-twentieth-century heyday, it was these days largely used as a depot for kayaks, a leaky inflatable dinghy, old jars of specimens in formaldehyde, ancient taxonomy books and classroom chairs with little writing desks attached. Fortunately, there were also some half-decent holding tanks with a still-functioning aeration system. Emma had worked hard the first year she was there, cleaning up the lab and restoring the tanks to working condition. They were conveniently segmented into individual compartments so that she could separate out her live specimens by species and health status. Carefully, she placed her sea stars and sea urchins into their respective tanks and allowed them to acclimate. When she set her water sample down on the salinity-testing counter at the other side of the lab, she felt the energy empty out of her as suddenly as the birds emptied the island. Her stomach rumbled. *Damn*, she thought. *Forgot to eat again.* Anxious to work and mildly irritated at the necessity of self-care, she walked up the big hill to the lighthouse kitchen to prepare a warm lunch.

The lighthouse was situated on the highest hill on the whole Gulf coast, from Key West to Texas. It served as a dormitory now, featuring several rooms with vinyl-mattress bunk beds, a full kitchen, and a small meeting room that could function as a classroom for school and research groups. These days, Emma lived much of the year in the lighthouse, engaged in research and avoiding people, especially hopeful suitors. She took her lunch out onto the dry-wood-planked back porch and sat down, surveying the island from the top down. She felt the energy of the land, something medicine woman Betty Mae Jumper had taught her to do in Big Cypress when she was very young. "Sit down, Emma," Betty Mae would instruct. "Settle in. Relax completely and close your eyes. What do you feel?" Emma closed her eyes, allowing her still-untouched lunch to cool on her lap. She felt the slightly disturbed breeze of a midday storm ruffling in from the north and east. She felt a heaviness too, one she had felt many times before, and she didn't know why.

Long before this island became the jewel of the Cedar Keys National Wildlife Refuge, way before the university built its marine laboratory there, and right before the lighthouse went up, the United States military used Seahorse Key as a Native American internment camp during the Seminole Wars. It was a brutal prison for her people, who were rounded up and held in this place of little fresh water or food and a plethora of highly venomous and unusually large cottonmouth snakes. There was a small cemetery behind the marine lab, but not for her people. The few old stone graves jutting up in the small clearing surrounded by beautyberry bushes, yaupon hollies, and small red cedars were marked for white sea captains and their families. But she knew that those of her ancestors who had died here from disease, mistreatment, dehydration, and malnourishment were now merged with the trees that surrounded the cemetery. These trees still grew and thrived, soaking up warmth and cold and breeze and stillness, eternally alive in oneness.

It was the way of her people, the people that had lived here for centuries before the first Spanish explorers arrived in

Florida in the 1500's, mapping and surveying both coasts with great interest. When in 1542 a Spanish cartographer named these keys the Islands of Cedars, *Las Islas Sabines,* Emma's direct descendants, the pre-Timucuan Potano peoples, were living here in harmony with the wild earth and sea in both life and death. The Spanish explorers by comparison found the jungled western Florida Gulf coast to be too challenging of an environment to settle in, and so found their hub instead in St. Augustine, making that Atlantic town the oldest in Florida. The descendants of these Spanish settlers, "Los Floridanos," eventually did migrate to other parts of Florida, including Cedar Key. To this day the Sanchez, Solana and Haven families, true Floridanos, have become well-established over many generations as fishermen, clammers, politicians, and more.

Emma considered her ancestors. After death, it was well known among here people that they were still here, alive and expanded in the trees, bearing witness to the coming of the Spanish and the Scotch-Irish and the African slaves. There was no need for a fabricated grave marker, for there was no boundary between life and death. So, when her more recent ancestors were brought here as prisoners, they still remembered how to die in Oneness, eternally holding space for all who came.

The heavy feeling, therefore, didn't make sense to her. It wasn't the way of her people. She knew that her ancestors were One now, they were Home. Choo-koh. Surrounded by the land and sea they merged with in life, merged also in death. But there was no mistaking the heaviness that was around her in the present, here, now. There had to be other souls nearby. Other souls who forgot how to come home. Perhaps they had been too long separated from the trees, too long oppressed and enslaved. She felt them more strongly when the breeze shifted and came directly from the east—from Way Key, the main island. And suddenly, she knew. There was only one group of people in these parts that had been torn from their homeland, bound, chained, and kept from freedom for generations, enough generations for their essence to separate from their home. She felt their despair, and felt her own tears swell. Their tears.

"Why, Ma Polly, why do I have this gift to know, but cannot help? What can I do?" she called out to the breeze, remembering her time ten years prior on Egmont Key as a graduate student. Egmont Key, another beautiful island boldly facing the open Gulf against the safety of the Tampa Bay estuary, had also been a holding prison for captured and enslaved Seminoles during the Third Seminole War. Like on Seahorse Key, the small cemetery there honors the memory of white soldiers and their families who were stricken with disease when they were stationed there, but Emma knew for a fact that the souls of at least seven Seminole prisoners who died there were resting peacefully as sabal palm trees. Still, she remembered feeling a heaviness there too, one related to the Civil War for sure but also something more recent, the suffering of what she now knew were African American souls still separated and lost.

While studying the echinoderms of Tampa Bay in the habitats around Egmont Key, Emma learned from her major professor about Seahorse Key, of which he spoke frequently and wistfully. As a Jewish scientist, her major professor was attuned to the horrors of persecution and sensitive to the travesty of the treatment of her people on both of these islands. He was also clearly more smitten with the remote Cedar Keys than the beautiful but heavily populated vacation paradise of Pinellas County. "It's in Levy County," he would tell her, "which was named after a Jewish man! Can you imagine, Emma, a successful Jew back in that time, here in the Deep South, when my grandparents were forced to flee their country just to survive!"

Inasmuch as Emma wanted to empathize with her professor's admiration of David Levy Yulee, however, it was a very difficult thing to do. Yulee was indeed Jewish, and his father Moses Elias Levy dreamed of working with him to create a new and peaceful Jewish settlement in Micanopy, near Gainesville. Moses abhorred slavery and persecution in all forms, and deemed that there would be no slavery or servitude allowed in Micanopy. But Levy Senior made one fatal error: in an effort to give young David a proper education, he sent his son to an upscale southern white boarding school. Surrounded and groomed by the white Christian confederacy during his formative years, young Levy Junior left his own tribe for the Confederate cause and its lure of fame and power.

David Levy Yulee renounced his father's dream of establishing Micanopy as a new Jewish settlement in Florida, open to all. Instead, he converted to Christianity (though he refused to get baptized), worked, manipulated, and married his way into Confederate Christian white society, and eventually became the state's first Jewish senator. He experienced lots of anti-Semitism along the way, and the more he did, the more his personal ambition drove him to defy his own heritage and his father's unpopular beliefs that slavery was wrong and that Jews, Africans, Native Americans, and others needed safe haven in inclusive settlements. Rather, in his quest for recognition and position, he perpetuated the idea that Florida should be a new white settlement, with railroads being the key to conquering the state. Despite doing everything he could save lightening his skin to appear less Sephardic, however, he still faced increasing prejudice as he became more and more successful. And, in some sort of dysfunctional counterbalance, in answer to the taunts about his nose and his skin, Levy pushed the Confederate cause even harder. He married the palest proper white Christian lady, had two children who received formal and very public baptisms, owned many slaves and vigorously pushed the institution of slavery, and became Florida's very first railroad baron.

In fact, at the very moment that Polly Parker was on that prison ship being unconscionably and uncomfortably chugged past Seahorse Key, two brothers–African slaves–were laboring in hot, mosquito-laden conditions in nearby Way Key to finish David Levy Yulee's Florida Railroad: the one that linked Fernandina Beach northeast of Jacksonville to the west coast, the one that was supposed to make Cedar Key a boomtown and Levy a very rich man. Dan Strong and his brother had been put to work by their owner, who was employed by Levy. Fortunately, the Strong brothers' owner was a kind man, not fully convinced by the common belief of the time that those of African descent were somehow less than human. After the railroad was completed, he granted both men their freedom.

The railroad that the Strongs helped to complete in Way Key never did thrive, as the Florida Railroad Company was re-organized and ultimately dissolved due to hardships throughout the Civil War. A different railroad linking the east coast of the state to Tampa in the west ended up being the successful one, leaving Cedar Key and Levy County in relatively remote obscurity. To add insult to injury, while Polly Parker was re-populating the Seminole Tribe, the Strong brothers' launched a soon-to-be successful freight business with the help of their former owner. The proceeds from that business helped Dan and his family settle on twenty-three acres in Otter Creek, and eventually the family would own land all over Florida. In the end, David Levy was immortalized only with a rural county named for him and the small Railroad Trestle Trail off State Road 24 on the way into Cedar Key. The trail bears a sign with his name and at the end of the short trail, hikers can still see the scattered posts that remain from the Strong brothers' hard work. Levy's great personal quest for power, in defiance of his own people's ill-treatment, fizzled with a failed railroad and obscurity, while the slaves who were forced to build it for him became respected and successful. In its own circuitous way, balance was restored.

Emma, still feeling the heaviness in the easterly breeze and the eerie absence of birds, considered the wisdom of balance she had inherited. The trees surrounding her, while small and salt-weathered, were old and wise. Anyone who understood the ways of balance knew that the overturning of life is just one continuum: we come from the earth and we continue through the trees, one universal existence, over and over again. We don't push or pull against it. We don't assert ourselves as something separate from it. All depends on this recognition of ecology and connection. When birds disappeared from Seahorse Key, cottonmouth snakes started eating each other. When pythons started eating all the other native species in the Everglades near where Emma had grown up, mega-flocks of crows started taking over. No one species is meant to lord over all the others. When it happens, it may seem that everything is ready to fall apart, but really it's the greater wheel that's overturning everything, awakening a return to balance. If Emma could help reinstitute balance, she would. She would study the sea stars and find out why they were sick. She would try to solve the mystery of the birds.

She would seek a way to help her deceased African American brothers and sisters merge with the trees. She wasn't sure how to do the latter one, so she asked the trees, and listened carefully.

They told her to eat her lunch.

Echinoderms

. . . .

There are a few types of advanced invertebrates that really give clues as to how our more evolved vertebrate systems might have developed. Sea stars, brittle stars, sea urchins, sea cucumbers, and sand dollars, which all belong to the phylum Echinodermata, are collectively known as echinoderms, and they belong in this important category. "Echinoderm" actually means "spiny skin," and true to their name, many echinoderms have some sort of subtle or conspicuous spiny outer covering.

The Cedar Keys are home to a rich variety of echinoderms, with a few species being the most common. In the seagrass beds, it's easy to find the sea stars *Echinaster sentus* and *Luidia clathrata* and the purple variegated sea urchin *Lytechinus variegatus*. On the sandbars, sand dollars *Mellita quinquiesperforata* var. *tenuis* are plentiful, and sea cucumbers *Allothyone mexicana* are regular helpful visitors to clam beds as they consume clam waste and keep the beds clean.

Echinoderms at first may seem fairly sedentary, but upon

closer inspection of the underside of any of the species, an observer will notice a complex hydraulic system of little tube feet that enable the animals to move via hydrostatic power, sometimes over long distances and with surprising efficiency. Tube feet are exclusive to this particular animal phylum.

As mentioned above, another thing that sets echinoderms apart from other invertebrates is their surprising physiological parallels to vertebrate systems. Their digestive, reproductive, and endocrine systems resemble much simpler versions of our own, and as such, scientists often use them to gain a better understanding of how our own physiology works. For example, one scientist discovered that echinoderms from the Cedar Keys and Tampa Bay contain levels of histamine in their digestive and reproductive organs that would make any mammal break out in hives. And yet, echinoderms don't have allergies or experience any other complications from these high levels of histamine. By exploring this phenomenon further, we might gain knowledge that helps us better regulate chronic allergies in humans.

In addition to their benefits as models for human medicine, echinoderms are vitally important for keeping the seagrass habitat in balance for the benefit of manatees, baby fish, and, ultimately, humans. People should never harvest them as souvenirs. When you see tourists collecting stacks of sand dollars and sea stars from a sandbar to dry out and take home, consider approaching them with compassion and raising their awareness about the important role echinoderms play in the ocean they so admire.

Chapter 9

THE BAOBAB TREE (2022)

THE SOIL CEREMONY was bittersweet for Jase. He hadn't been to Rosewood in a very long time, not since he and his family had driven by the little green sign on Highway 24 on their regular commutes between Gainesville and Cedar Key. Growing up, he had heard the stories of his Great-grandpa Sam and how his granddad had an idyllic childhood in the fertile hammocks that were his backyard. That is, until the freezing night when it all ended in shots, screams, and flames. He heard a lot about the big oak tree too, the one that his great grandfather hung machinery on while his granddad clambered throughout the gently curving, Spanish-moss-dripping arms of its lower branches. His granddad was never hungry, he told Jase, and never lonely, because Rosewood was a village in the truest sense, where people took care of each other.

Unlike many African Americans in Florida who arrived as escaped antebellum-era slaves by way of the Carolinas or as the progeny of freed slaves seeking work, Jase's family's path was a near-direct traverse from the African homeland. His Great-grandpa Sam's grandfather was a Jola fisherman from West Africa, the last in a Senegalese family line that spanned centuries until the slave trade arrived on their shores. Sam's grandfather was lucky enough to have been on a slave ship whose human cargo successfully revolted halfway across the Atlantic. After killing their captors and tossing them overboard as bull shark chum near the Caribbean, the able-bodied

West African seamen navigated to the lush island of Antigua, where most settled and lived peaceful lives. Sam's grandfather never stopped dreaming of Senegal, however, and not realizing that slavery had finally been abolished in Senegal in the mid-nineteenth-century, he resented the fact that his homeland had become unsafe and unavailable to him. As a young man, he wasn't content to settle down on a small island. So he hopped a boat to south Florida, eager for some sort of adventure to allay his longings. In south Florida he found kinship with the Seminoles and lots of work. As the years went on, he married a Seminole woman and lived a nomadic life, gaining skills and following available labor-based jobs in fishing, turpentine, and logging up the state. Eventually, he gave up his lifelong kinship with the sea in favor of greater job security in the expansive forests of north Florida, where he settled down and learned the blacksmithing trade. He passed on his skills to his son, who passed them on to Sam.

Sam's grandfather talked wistfully about Senegal throughout his lifetime, and Sam loved to hear his many stories. He especially loved the way his grandfather spoke about the mysterious baobab tree in a lilting and melodic African accent that made the experience seem even more magical, like the tree itself. "The tree is upside down," his grandfather would say, "like the roots are in the sky. It is to remind us that our roots are connected to the heavens, in one continuous loop. We are not separate, young Sam. Look at this oak tree. See how the roots spread widely and deeply into the ground? See how the branches look the same? Remember the baobab, young Sam. It is one with this oak tree, with all trees, and with YOU."

Sam passed his grandfather's stories on to his own son and grandson, who passed them on to Jase. While Jase had never been to Africa, these stories and traditions were part of his very cells. He became fascinated with the ways in which our ancestors shaped the present and the future, and in particular how our timeless connection to the earth herself could be the lifeline that keeps something infinitely alive through the constant overturning of life and death, generation after generation. This same fascination is what had kept him mesmerized as an adolescent by the tunicates and glass eels in Cedar Key. When his father was brutally assaulted, causing his family to up and move permanently to Archer, he felt as if that vital lifeline had been severed. It wasn't just the separation from his best friend, Roy, and his having been forbidden to spend time on the island "for his own safety." It was much bigger than that. It had to do with the color of his skin and his access to wild, free spaces and his ability to exist as one with them. It had to do with things that should never be forbidden, things that were by natural design meant to be one in their very diversity, not ever meant to be separated.

Jase did well in Archer. After graduating from the magnet program at his high school, he was easily admitted with scholarships into the honors program at University of Florida in nearby Gainesville–as he had once told Roy he would be–and then went on to a graduate program in African American studies. For his Ph.D., he delved deeply into origin stories of African Americans, and those in Florida in particular. He was enthralled to discover that the African diaspora was as diverse and widespread as those of Jews, Mexicans and Vietnamese, with the added complexities of hundreds of distinct African tribes, languages and dialects and unique groups like the Creoles and their bicoastal language and history. Because of his Florida upbringing, he was perhaps most interested in the cultural evolution of blacks of the American Deep South who, though separated by many generations from the African motherland, were steeped in a soulful, spiritual, culture rooted in deep wounds and a resilience of spirit all their own.

Graduate school is where Jase met his beloved wife Sofia. She was working on her Ph.D. in Latin American women's studies with an emphasis on the modern-day influence of legendary South American female powerhouses such as Argentina's Evita Peron, Brazil's Maria Leopoldina, and Ecuador's Manuela Saenz. Both Jase and Sofia were on the organizing committee for the first annual Social Justice Awareness Day event on campus. They were excited to be on the front lines of a movement inspired by the great Reverend Martin Luther King Junior, one that had gone stagnant in recent years in the Deep South as a rampant and insidious new kind of prejudice, much more difficult to identify and set right, crept in to maintain the system of inequality. Both Jase and Sofia had spent years of their lives identifying this new "microaggression" and were determined to bring awareness to it, to update the social justice movement to include not only people of color but also any and all peoples subject to micro- and macro-aggressions. Their mutual passion for social justice soon grew into an equally mutual passion for one another.

After successfully defending their dissertations, they married and tried to have a baby. Three traumatic miscarriages later, they gave up attempting to expand their family and instead focused their energies on raising awareness and developing sensitivity in their next generation of students. For a decade, they were deeply in love and proactive in their work together in their classroom and the wider world. They authored papers and essays together, and were often invited to speak at universities all over the world. One day, when they were packing up materials for their keynote presentation at the Social Justice, Equity, and Inclusion Symposium at the

University of California in Los Angeles, Sofia started feeling unwell.

"It's just a cold, I think, mi amor, and I'm un poco nauseous," Sofia reassured Jase in her alluring Peruvian Spanglish. "You go without me, hmmm? I'll be okay." Jase was concerned, as Sofia was rarely sick, but this was a huge symposium that was garnering a lot of media attention, and they both reasoned it would be best if at least one of them were there to represent their work. He reluctantly kissed her goodbye and set off for the airport.

When he returned a week later, Sofia was in the hospital. Two days and countless tests later, the doctors gravely informed them that she had a rare and inoperable neuroendocrine tumor–the worst the oncologist had ever seen–and it had metastasized aggressively. Sofia died one week later in Jase's arms, and his whole world collapsed.

Standing there now underneath the big oak tree, he suddenly remembered the first time he brought Sofia to Rosewood. They just stood together in silence for the longest time, facing inward towards the inaccessible hammock. A flock of majestic white pelicans flew overhead, bound for the Gulf. When he looked over at her, tears were cascading down her cheeks, and he loved her all the more.

She would have been so proud of this moment in Rosewood, he knew, when the victims were at last being offered acknowledgment, and their descendants, like Jase, along with kindred spirits in peace and justice work were gathering together more and more to literally dig up the past and bring injustice to light in the most honorable and dignified of ways.

"Sofia," Jase said softly to himself, "I wish you were here." Since her death, he had mourned by pouring himself into his work, their work, but had managed to avoid quiet ceremonial moments in which he might be forced to fully acknowledge his loss.

I miss you, mi cielo. Mi amor.

He felt turned upside down, like the baobab tree. Maybe at least this way he could be somehow connected to her, with his roots facing the heavens. "Baobab," Jase mouthed in the euphonic way that his father had taught him. He pondered the regal live oak his granddaddy once climbed up, swung from, and rested upon as a small child, and it appeared to him like an ancient and ageless caregiver, with nurturing arms extending equally to the heavens and into the ground, inviting something familiar to him. The soil ceremony was taking place in the shade of this great oak, and Jase knew that this fact would be meaningful to both Sofia and his great-grandfather, whose body had dangled from these branches above the spot where silver ceremonial spoons agitated the dirt.

"Damn shame," came a voice from behind him. Startled, Jase whirled around to see an attractive middle-aged woman, dressed in boyfriend jeans and a casual T-shirt. She looked so unlike the well-heeled attendees with their colorful clothes, some in African prints and others dressed, as if for Sunday sermon, in pastel frocks and church-worthy wide brimmed hats.

"Excuse me?" responded Jase, his reverie broken.

"Damn shame, what happened here. Coulda happened where I live, but they passed us by, you know." She extended out a lean, cocoa-colored arm for a handshake. "Alberta Strong, from Otter Creek. Nice to meet you."

Jase's eyebrows lifted in recognition as he shook her hand. "The Strong family! Of course! Nice to meet you, Alberta. Your family's name holds a hella lot of respect where I come from."

"That so?" Alberta replied, pleased. "And where is it you

come from, 'xactly?"

"Well," Jase said, "right here, specifically. I mean, I live in Gainesville now, but my great-granddaddy, Sam Carter, was hung from this very tree. You know, he knew your great-grandparents, the Strongs of Otter Creek, and my daddy said y'all are good folks. Glad to see that unlike all of us Rosewood people, y'all are still around."

Alberta's face dimmed. "Your great-granddaddy was Sam Carter? Oh, Lord." She paused for a minute, considering the whole picture. "The Klan came right in to Otter Creek, you know, ready to murder all the black folk, but the whites encouraged them to keep goin'. They told 'em it was the blacks in Rosewood that needed the beating, not us. The whites in Otter Creek needed the black folk, you know, to keep things in order, what with all the cleanin' and farmin' and labor that needed to be done. Lord knows they didn't wanna do it, y'hear? I sure as hell don't." Jase couldn't help but laugh at her edgy candor.

She continued, "But to this day my family feels sad about it, because we all did well, you know? Right from the time my great-great-grandaddy Dan Strong became a free man, we got all the breaks. We own tons of land. But not the seven Rosewood families. The Klan was madder'n hell by the time they got here, havin' made up some reason to do what they done, and now, well, here we are today finally recognizing it. But you never got your land back. All because of one horrific week and many lifetimes of inhumanity." She paused and looked around, surveying the crowd. "I am glad you're here, Jase. Maybe you can help me understand something: Where did all the survivors from Rosewood end up goin' after they escaped here?"

"Well, I know my great-grandma and granddad froze near

to death in their nightclothes for two nights in the swamp while all the houses and the churches and other buildings burned. They were rescued with other women and children by a train bound for Archer and Gainesville. That's where I grew up, Archer. And I know some other descendants in Archer, but everyone else is farther away, like Lacoochee and south Florida and Tampa and even other states. Everybody just ran. Don't feel guilty about it, Alberta. It woulda been that much worse if your family was attacked too. I'm glad some black folks from this part of the world got some good luck for a change, and hey, we're all okay now."

"Some of us are doing okay, sure, but man, we got a ways to go, you know? I mean, seventy years to put up a small sign and pay some small reparations? One hundred years to have a soil ceremony with only one local newspaper covering it? Confederate war hero statues at every city hall in any direction? Black brothers and sisters on the news 'bout every day, gettin' shot and strangled going out for a run or a soda or even just sleeping? Maybe the Otter Creek Strongs had a smoother ride compared to the families from Rosewood, but even I still don't dare walk down the street by myself."

Jase looked at her admiringly. "Dang, girl, you tell it like it is, don't you?"

"Damn straight I do." They caught each other's eyes and held them for a few very enjoyable seconds.

The growing magnetism between them was quickly severed as a huge red pickup truck trailing a new Grady-White fishing boat roared its engines on Highway 24, slowing down in front of the Rosewood sign. The ball-capped, blue-eyed driver gunned his truck repeatedly as he shouted from the truck's open window, "BLACKS GO HOME!" He raised a thick forearm, brightly tattooed with bald eagles encircling the U.S.

flag, and curled his fingers into a "fuck you."

Jase's countenance fell. With one obnoxious rev of a truck's engine, one ignorant yowl that wholly contained centuries worth of aggression and oppression, he suddenly didn't feel like a respected professor of history anymore. He held his breath reflexively, an ancient response to danger. His gut clenched in a too-familiar sensation of fear and despair, and he was a little boy again with a broken and bleeding father and a wounded spirit, wondering, over and over again, "What did we do wrong to make you hate us so much?"

The truck circled back for a second attack. "BLACK SCUM! GIT THE HELL OUT! GO HOME!" The driver pulled the truck into the gravel parking area with a dramatic screech, and another, smaller truck and its equally white, tattooed, and ball-capped driver pulled in right beside. A mob of two.

Jase felt terror, and then anger. He looked at Alberta, connecting again with her now-fearful eyes, and turned into the uneasy silence that had fallen over the frozen crowd standing under his great-granddaddy's big oak. Each person in the crowd wore a familiar look of ingrained dread.

Jase watched as the two men approached the gathering, then looked up at the tree, inspired by its unmoving calm.

"We *are* home," he stated to the universe, and exhaled, trusting that he would somehow figure out what to do next.

Live Oaks and Spanish Moss

Just as alligators and manatees are synonymous with Florida, so does the image of live oaks draped in Spanish moss conjure thoughts of the sultry American Deep South. This floral pairing is especially abundant in northern Florida, where conditions are ideal for a perfect live oak/moss partnership.

The southern live oak (*Quercus virginiana*) can reach one hundred feet in height, and the crowns of the oldest trees can expand to half the size of a football field. Long-lived, they are the "redwoods of the southeast," living for hundreds upwards to a thousand years when left alone. Unfortunately, live oaks were once logged for their sturdy wood. The famous naval ship *U.S.S. Constitution* was nicknamed "Old Ironsides" during the War of 1812 because its live-oak hull stood up to repeated cannon fire.

The largest of the live oaks are known as "champion trees," as they are critical to biodiversity and climate stability. Unlike other species of oak trees, live oaks are evergreen, providing a habitat for a large number of vertebrate and invertebrate species. Spanish moss tends to favor older, larger live oaks, which are full of anchoring substrate and humidity which the epiphytes need to thrive.

Spanish moss (*Tillandsia usneoides*) is neither Spanish nor a moss. In the Bromeliad family, it is much more closely related to pineapples. Its name came from a back-and-forth name-calling feud between the French explorers and Spanish conquistadors of old. The French decided the hairlike strands reminded them of Spanish beards, so they called the plant *barb Espagnol*, or Spanish beard. The Spanish retorted that the hanging plants much more closely resembled unkempt French hair, and called it cabello Frances, or French hair. Ultimately, the insult to the Spanish prevailed, and to this day the draping Bromeliad is commonly referred to as Spanish beard or Spanish moss.

Both live oaks and the Spanish moss they host are important for the ecology. Rat snakes and several species of bats live in Spanish moss, and birds love to use the strands for their nests. In fact, during the Civil War, Spanish moss was big business due to its fibrous qualities. It was used as everything from mattress stuffing to insulation to thread for sewing. The profuse Bromeliad is also a favorite nesting place for chiggers, aka redbugs, aka the itchiest and most aggravating bugs in Florida. It is not recommended that you pull down the long strands and put them on your head like a wig, for example.

Chapter Ten

SHARKS, BIRDS, AND SEA STARS (2022)

OF ALL THE days to have to go to Gainesville, Roy muttered to himself in irritation. But he had to go to the VA Hospital for his annual physical, pick up his Ma's prescriptions, and take his car in for servicing–and it had all taken way longer than he'd expected. And now, thanks to one obnoxious jerk driving an overloaded truck in front of him, he would be late for his date at 29 North: his first date in maybe forever, his first date having only one leg, and definitely his first date with a goddess. They were meeting at Emma's favorite restaurant at 7pm, it was already 6:30, and he had twenty-three more goddam miles to go.

He had been stuck behind this asshole since Otter Creek on State Road 24, the single road that extends for those twenty-three more miles to Cedar Key. The guy was hauling a new 32-foot Grady White, almost too big and drafty for Cedar Key, but a boat that Roy would've bought in a snap anyways if he'd had that kind of money. The truck hauling the boat was shiny, red, large, and looked familiar. The dick driving it seemed to delight in slowing down until Roy tried to pass him and then flooring it just as Roy started to switch lanes. Roy very much wanted to beat in the driver's entitled, obnoxious head, but he'd learned the rough and stupid way not to engage with guys as jacked-up on testosterone as this one clearly was; and the moron was clearly rich to boot. Roy had way too much to lose, so he dropped Emma a quick "stuck in traffic" text, put some space between him and the truck, and surrendered to his daydreams. *Emma.*

Quickly, his mood morphed from frustration to reverie as he focused on why he was in such a hurry to get back to Cedar Key. He needed to find out if it was actually a dream that she was meeting him for dinner, drinks, conversation...*more*? He wouldn't make the mistake of expecting the "more" part, not after what it took just to get the date in the first place. Still, he felt plenty warm as he recalled the events of the week before, during the no-name storm.

He was halfway between his clam tracts and Seahorse Key when the storm let loose, so he was planning to skip check-ing his shark buoys and just shelter on the island until the weather passed. But when he set his binoculars on the buoys, he was surprised to see two of them bobbing up and down, demonstrably tethered to large and angry fish. *Sharks on!* As rain pummeled his cheeks, he gaffed the buoys and hauled up two good-sized elasmobranchs: one blacktip and one bull. But even through the rain, he could immediately see these wouldn't be for eating. The scientists needed to know about the big, oozing lesions they had on their backs. They were clearly sick.

The storm fully unloaded on him as he pulled into the Seahorse Key marine lab dock. He grabbed the sharks by their tail pits and dragged them up a small hill to the lab. Soaked through and now shivering, with two hands full of unhealthy sharks, he kicked the door open and walked into the welcome shelter.

The lab was dark. He dropped the weakly flailing sharks to the floor and reached for the switch. Nothing. Storm must've tripped the electricity, but that was okay. He just needed a moment to catch his breath, dry off, rest a minute, and find a place to situate the sharks and give the ranger a call to let him know what he had brought, maybe find a scientist or Captain Kenny at the lighthouse to come and take a look. He slid into one of the classroom chair-desks and rested his wet head on his tattooed arms.

"Can I help you?"

The voice was soft but startled him so completely that he tipped the chair and fell backwards. He toppled on top of the two gasping sharks, shrieked, and jumped up. But the floor was so slick with the water he'd tracked in that he slipped backwards and fell onto his butt, yelling, "GOSHDAMOW-WWWITTT!"

Emma couldn't help herself. Even in the low light she recognized him as the oaf in the bird dog from earlier that afternoon, but the scene was so ridiculous that a professional comic would've been hard pressed to mimic it. She busted out laughing. Wholly disarmed, with eyes adjusted to the dim, Roy at once realized that he was in the lab with the woman he'd made a fool of himself over earlier, and her laughter felt like a sensuous waterfall. While she guffawed, he melted. He tried to compose himself, soaking on the floor, flanked by two suffering sharks. He attempted a smooth start to conversation. "It's you! The lady from earlier today! Say, you're not from around here, are you?"

Oh god, no, I did NOT just ask that, did I? Roy was disgusted with himself.

The laughter stopped. Emma's soft voice contained a slight edge as she replied, "I certainly am, and for about twenty generations longer than you."

Roy, blinking, seemed genuinely puzzled, so she filled in the blanks for him. "I'm Native American. Seminole tribe, but my lineage goes all the way back to the Potano peoples. Been here just a bit longer than you and your kin, in other words." She now seemed annoyed. "Is the storm almost over?" She looked out the window hopefully, and he could not mistake how her expression fell when she realized that the weather was worsening and would be for a while, leaving her stuck in his company for longer than she would like. He clearly wasn't her type. He was afraid to say anything more, so he was relieved when Emma's gaze fell to the sharks. "Whoa!" she exclaimed. "What did you bring here? Look at those specimens!"

An opening. Roy replied, "Yea, I just caught 'em, between here and Snake Key, y'know? I had buoys set, because I've been hired to survey and capture sharks with diseases, and bring them in, y'know?" He paused, feeling proud of his status. "But this is the first time I've seen you here. I mean, usually I bring 'em to Nature Coast Biological, but there was no way I was gonna drive through this hellfire of a storm, y'know? So I was hoping I could bring 'em here, y'know? Even though I don't really know much about this lab and all. Y'know?" *Jesus, how many times am I going to say "y'know?"*

Emma smiled despite herself. He was so nervous. "What's your name?" she ventured.

"Roy. Roy Bamford. Third-generation fisherman, Cedar Key. What's yours?"

"Emma. Emma Tiger. Marine invertebrate biologist, researcher and professor. Well, Roy, it seems the storm did us both a favor, because these sharks have a similar kind of pathology as the sea stars I was collecting earlier today, when we first, um, met."

Roy's mortification began to dissipate as he became genuinely interested. "Really? No kidding? Can I see?"

Emma was surprised and somewhat disarmed at his sudden transition from bumbling suitor to someone with a genuine scientific interest in her work. She could meet him there. "Yes, of course! Come on over to these tanks. Whoa, watch your step...!" She extended a hand as Roy stumbled on the puddled floor. He held on as he eased himself up to standing, enjoying the sensation of her hand in his. Then, catching her surprised look when she saw where the hem of his jeans had hiked up his leg enough to expose the shin of his prosthetic, he pulled his hand away self-consciously. The look she gave him was one of unexpected compassion, but he quickly dismissed it as pity. *Great. On top of everything else, she's disgusted by my deformity. Another strike. What next?*

He walked with her over to the other side of the lab, where she aimed her flashlight over the holding tanks and explained, "See? These are healthy *Luidia* and *Echinaster*, two common species of sea stars that live around here in the seagrass beds. But in this tank over here, we've got specimens of the same two species with lesions that look a lot like the ones on your sharks over there. They don't move as well and they don't eat as much. There is definitely something going on in our waters that is increasingly causing both invertebrates and vertebrates to show this type of dermal pathology."

"Dermal what now?" responded Roy, but then seemed to understand. "Oh! Skin disease!" he deduced triumphantly. Emma seemed pleased too, so he asked, "But why? Why do you think marine animals are getting skin diseases?"

"Well, there is a bigger story that might be unfolding here," offered Emma. "You know about the birds here on Seahorse Key, right?"

"Only that submarines, an escaped pet circus monkey, too many raccoons, and covert military helicopter operations scared 'em all away in 2015, and they never came back," Roy replied.

Emma couldn't help herself, and again laughed out loud. Roy was a little embarrassed, because, while it was a very attractive laugh, it also indicated that she believed he was full of shit. Nonetheless, she endeavored to soften her tone. "Well, yes, those are all some theories. But think about it. The water is too shallow here for submarines." *Well duh.* Roy knew that. "Folks have combed every square meter of this island and there is definitely no monkey here, and it's not exactly overrun by raccoons, either. As for the helicopters doing military ops or looking for drug runners, well, yes, that may have been a factor. But it couldn't be the only factor. Maybe just a tipping point."

Roy became thoughtful. Somehow, this bird-abandonment mystery must be tied in with the sick sharks and sea stars, or else she wouldn't have brought it up. He ventured, "So, it's somehow connected to what's happening to the marine animals we're finding?"

"Well, that's what I'm wondering," replied Emma, surprised to find herself now enjoying her conversation with this version of Roy. "It's the focus of my research now, and I'm exploring factors like salinity change and water temperature. It seems more likely, especially after reading research on other bird-abandonment events in other parts of the world, that there has been a gradual lessening of optimal conditions for the birds, and so they were already skittish. Something like low-flying drug-busting helicopters might have just been the final straw. And if we ever want them to come back, it would be a good idea to see what other longer-term factors are at play."

In a surge of confidence, partially fueled by the fact he

was feeling a lot more comfortable and authentically wanted to talk about this subject some more, he asked Emma out
right then and there. "The storm's dying down, and I gotta get
back to the city dock and check on my Ma. She's sick, and she
doesn't like storms. Can we continue this conversation again
soon, maybe over dinner?"

And to his surprise, she responded, "Yes."

Pelicans

It's an exciting time of year in the Cedar Keys when the American white pelicans (*Pelecanus erythrorhyncos*) arrive in elegant, V-shaped flocks for their winter vacation. With a nine-and-a-half-foot wingspan, they are easily one of North America's largest birds, sporting black-tipped wings and peach-colored bills, legs, and toes. They are literally snowbirds, spending the rest of the year in areas as far north as Canada. The year-round resident brown pelicans (*Pelicanus occidentalis*) don't seem to mind their seasonal company. Brown pelicans nest in trees and mangroves, while white pelicans make nests right on the ground. Brown pelicans are famous for their dramatic air dives and head shakes to catch their fish, while white pelicans simply paddle around on the surface of the water, sometimes even working cooperatively to corral the fish, and then submerge their heads and open their flexible bills to catch them. They are both content to live in parallel, the presence of neither causing much change to their daily routines.

Both species, however, are canaries in the coal mine when it comes to environmental distress. Pesticides cause direct death as well as eggshell thinning and resulting reproductive failure. While pesticide regulations and relative lack of pesticides in the Cedar Keys National Wildlife Refuge has reduced this threat, pelicans are still chronically subject to injury and death by fishing lines and hooks, and are increasingly affected by sea-level rise and habitat encroachment.

Chapter 11
REUNION (2022)

IT WAS 7PM, date-with-Emma time, and Roy was now only nine miles from the restaurant. He was still stuck behind the jerk, who'd just slowed way down to shout out his window at a large group of well-dressed, mostly African American folks gathered just to the south of the Rosewood memorial sign. Roy was determined to pass. He tailgated the jerk so close, he could make out the peeling "Bronson Speedway" sticker on his back windshield. He was gonna pass now. But wait—*What the hell?* The driver had drifted over into the lane of oncoming traffic, tattooed arm sticking way out, middle finger waving maliciously at the dignified-looking group. Roy was both curious and worried. Clearly, these were respectable folks engaged in some sort of ceremony at the Rosewood site. Everyone knew what happened at Rosewood, even if no one ever talked about it, and it wasn't uncommon to see groups of people by the memorial sign. He'd heard they traveled from all over the country to pay their respects, take pictures, and offer remembrances. Even his pa, loose cannon that he was, wouldn't fly his racist flag unless he was over-the-top drunk. This guy wasn't driving like he was that far gone. So what was he doing? Roy put his window down in time to hear, "FUCK-ING TRESPASSERS! GET YOUR BLACK ASSES OUTTA HERE! GO HOME!"

Roy hadn't liked the moron since Otter Creek, but this be-havior crossed the line. The back of his head started getting hot, usually a sign he was about to do something stupid. He forgot about his own safety and honked his horn, waving the man on to get him to leave it alone already. But instead, the jerk seemed to take this gesture–coming from another ball-capped and tattooed white guy driving another pickup–as a call to arms. So, rather than driving on by, he pulled into the small parking area by the sign. *Shit!* thought Jase, now on full alert and equally full of protective bravado. *What the hell is he doing? He can't do this!* And then Roy saw them--the plastic testicles, swinging from the trailer hookup. *Awwwwwww, man....It's the boat ramp alpha dude. Well shit. Shit shit shit. I guess I gotta deal with this dude after all.*

Roy pulled in beside the testicle-bedecked truck, and locked his eyes on the driver. The red-faced, blue-eyed man seemed encouraged by Roy's "mean look," and gazed back at him knowingly, like they shared a secret. "Hey man, thanks for havin' my back," he said. "My name's Clemson Dawes. You?"

It made Roy sick to see that this Clemson Dawes identified him as one of this man's own, especially since he seemed to think Roy was volunteering to be his sidekick in harassment or worse. He had to cool this guy down. "I'm Roy. Hey man, leave these nice folks alone, all right? They ain't causin' no one no trouble."

Clemson Dawes's visage reddened further, changing im-mediately from an expression of kinship to one of enraged disappointment. "Like hell! This is private, white man's prop-erty! They got no right to come trespassin' here! I'm callin' the police! Hell, I'm kickin' 'em out myself!"

Jase, who was within earshot, felt emboldened when he realized that the other man was there to defuse, not incite. He stepped forward and called out, "Actually, sir, we got per-mission from the property owners here. They gave us their blessing and their support, and...wait...Roy?"

Roy was so focused on trying to rein in the caveman who reminded him so much of his father that when he turned to look at the African American man who'd just called him by name, he didn't, right at first, recognize his long lost friend. But then he exclaimed, "Jase! Jase! My God man, where have you been?" and the two immediately embraced.

This was all too much for Clemson Dawes. "Really now? Fuck you all!" He spat at the gathering, "This ain't your land, y'hear?" He then directed a sharp gaze at Roy. "And you, you N-lover. I got your head on my tally, y'hear? I ever see you by yourself, you're DEAD, asshole. Fuckin' traitor."

But Roy and Jase were so overjoyed to see each other that the man with the truck nuts held no power over them, at least not in that precious moment of recognition and reunion. Their fear melted under the warmth of boyhood solidarity. In synchronicity, they both raised their middle fingers at Clem Dawes and his scarlet face. Clem whirled away in a vortex of expletives and maximized every ability his truck had to break decibel levels as he peeled out and scorched west towards Cedar Key.

The boyhood friends turned back towards one another.

"Jase!" exclaimed Roy.

"Roy!" answered Jase.

Roy appraised Jase admiringly. "Man, look at you! You look so...professor-like! You look freakin' great!"

Jase beamed as he responded, "And you look good too. You actually look the same, man....Just taller, and your hair's turnin' gray! Almost didn't recognize you at first, but I heard you talking to that dude, man, and your voice sounded familiar. It made me look closer." They slapped each other's back and embraced again.

Suddenly, both men became aware that the eyes of the crowd had turned to them with a collective gaze of warmth and relief. Roy and Jase could almost hear the whole group exhale. The elder matriarch, however, looked stern. "Excuse me, gentlemen," she said, "Thank you both for standing up for us. But we have had enough interruptions on this important day. We were just preparing to light candles for the seven family branches who once lived here, before that awful week one hundred years ago. Kindly take your conversation elsewhere, so we may conclude this sacred ceremony before dark?"

Roy and Jase nodded synchronously and offered a thumbs up, feeling like boys again, trying to stifle a giggle at being hushed. Just like the old days. Like no time had passed at all. The two of them moved as one unit, sneaking off to the side. "Stay, man," implored Jase. "The ceremony is about half over. I'd love for you to see it."

Suddenly, Roy felt out of place, and he also remembered Emma waiting for him at 29 North. "Thanks, man, but I don't think I belong here."

"Course you do, man! You're not anything like that asshole." Roy flinched. Jase, understanding, ventured further. "Hey, you're not your father. You're my friend. And I've really missed you. Didn't even realize how much until now."

Roy was deeply moved by Jase's sentiment. It had been many years, yet they were at total ease with one another, as if decades and hurt and heartache hadn't passed. Roy understood that Jase was still his best friend, the kind you have for life if you're lucky. So, his answer was equally open: "I'm ashamed of my pa, and I'm ashamed of that Clemson guy, and I would gladly stay if it helped. But this, right here, this is your family's history, man. This is the past. Your great-grandfather died here. You're here to honor him and Rosewood. Don't let me distract you from that. And let's not let all that shit keep us from being friends anymore. Can you meet me later tonight in Cedar Key? I actually have a date at 29 North and she's waiting for me...."

Jase didn't miss a beat. "Oooh-hoooo! A date! I knew you'd end up being a ladies man!"

"SHHHHHH!" shushed the group's matriarch, and the two men again stifled guffaws.

"No, no, Jase, it ain't like that at all. Shit, I haven't had so much as a girlfriend since comin' back from Desert Storm." Jase looked surprised, realizing he didn't even know that Roy had served. "Man, there's SO much to tell you. But if you can come out there, meet me there in like two hours, we can sit at the bar and catch up. And you can meet her too! That is if I don't blow it....Man, I'm sweatin'. I ain't been on a date in over a stinkin' decade."

Jase toned down the chaffing, and met Roy where he was.. "I got you, man. Okay then. I'll see you in two hours. We got so much to catch up on. But at least stay for the candle lighting. Just five minutes more. My personal history or not, it's important for all of us to acknowledge the families that once lived here. It would mean something for you to stay and see it. You know, many of these folks here today are descended from at least one of the families. We're all finding each other after all these years, finally talking about it. Rosewood is more than just a memory, man."

Roy was touched, and despite how little he actually knew about the details of Rosewood and his anxiousness to get to Emma, he found himself deeply moved over the next few minutes as the woman lit seven candles and the group reverently called out each family name in turn.

Bradley. Carrier. Coleman. Edwards. Evans. Goins. Hall. Rob-

inson.

The men embraced a third time. Then Jase returned to the ceremony, and Roy drove to Emma's favorite restaurant.

Water Moccasins
....

Florida is an ideal habitat for a diverse selection of venomous and nonvenomous snakes. Of the venomous species, perhaps the water moccasin (*Agkistrodon conanti*) deserves the most caution and respect. Anyone who spends time around any body of water in the state is well advised to learn to distinguish this snake from the eight species of harmless water snakes (genus *Nerodia*) that both closely resemble the water moccasin and share similar distribution and habitat.

The most distinctive difference is that, as pit vipers, moccasins have a conspicuous pit organ between their nose and eyes. The eyes themselves are another helpful clue, with the moccasins' being slanted with cat-like, vertical pupils, while the non-venomous water snakes have round, black pupils. The moccasins' most famous characteristic, however, is that when they feel threatened, they open their mouth to reveal a bright white interior, earning them the alternate name of cottonmouth. Though their venom is potent, cottonmouths are generally not aggressive, and are unlikely to bite unless harassed or stepped upon.

Most water moccasins require a source of fresh water to survive, making the once-thriving population of many hundreds of these snakes on Seahorse Key an enigma for many years. Scientists studying the unique ecology of the island discovered a symbiotic relationship between the cottonmouths and the fish-eating bird species, wherein the snakes depended on the dregs and droppings of the birds. When the birds mysteriously abandoned Seahorse Key in 2015, the cottonmouth population suffered tremendously, eventually resorting to cannibalism. The cottonmouth population has since decreased dramatically, and ecologists can only hope that with a gradual return of birds to the island, the unique ecology and trophic relationships of this island will be restored. As with so many other species that are potentially dangerous to humans, it is important to remember that encounters resulting in harm to humans are actually very rare, and these animals are critical to maintaining the balance of our delicate ecosystems.

Chapter 12
FIRST DATE (2022)

EMMA WAS WAITING at a table that overlooked the Gulf of Mexico, with Atsena Odie in clear view. Sunset was definitely the best time of the day to be at this very spot. It was 7:45, and according to his texts, Roy was held up behind slow-moving traffic, but she didn't mind. She had already enjoyed a phenomenal day in the embrace of Florida's wilderness, having experienced a rare alligator sighting in the backwaters where she docked her boat after coming in from Seahorse Key. The fair-sized gator was just cruising along, unphased by the change in salinity and likely attracted by the lure of dinner all around in the fertile nursery waters. Now, she was settling into an intimate date with the sunset, which presented itself as a backdrop of purples and oranges that glinted off the backs of leisurely rolling dolphins and wisps of playful post-storm clouds. To be concerned with Roy's late arrival would sabotage this moment, what her mom used to call "the only now you'll ever have." But, she contemplated, how could she "have" it? As she was enjoying this moment, she didn't have a sense that she had anything at all, that these miraculous things could belong to her or anyone. The colors, the dolphins, the clouds, and she were simply part of one dance.

She heard the chair across from her slide along the floor, and caught sight of Roy in her peripheral vision, dropping heavily into the seat. "So sorry to keep you waiting," offered Roy, slightly out of breath from hopping up the stairs to the dining room two at a time. Emma turned her eyes reluctantly from the picture window and surveyed Roy. He looked like he'd had a long and weary day, and she couldn't help but wonder if it was more than just traffic that had made him late. She could also read the hint of disappointment in his face: that he wasn't on time, that he hadn't had time to change, that he started their first date late, breathless, and disheveled. She kind of liked the veritable Roy. She hoped he would stay as authentic as he appeared right now, that he wouldn't try to play it cool.

Well, a girl could dream. Almost before she'd had time to finish the thought, Roy, attempting to sit up straight and play down his obvious fatigue, said jauntily, "Well, aren't you a sight for sore eyes...."

Really? Emma didn't want to waste her time here. And she definitely didn't want a date that started off with worn-out lines about how she looked. She had come here to get to know the fisherman who'd finally gotten waterlogged enough to let his guard down and reveal his fascination with the sharks, the sea stars, the sunset. Was he here? "Listen, Roy," she ventured bluntly. "Don't use platitudes on me, okay? Let me be frank. I just got over a bad breakup, and I'm too heartbroken and too old to be interested in playing games. But I could use a nice person to talk to. Can we do that?"

Roy was flummoxed. Here he was, trying to put on a "can of man" like his pa used to tell him he had to do with the ladies. Not only was he grossly out of practice, but as he suddenly recalled, it had never really seemed to work anyway. She didn't like it, and he liked her. He had to figure out how to be himself. And he had to say something. "Uh, okay."

"So what happened out there on the road today?" Emma queried. "Sunday evenings aren't typically rush hour on State

Road 24." Roy suddenly wanted to tell her everything...about the Bronson bonehead named Clemson Dawes, the ceremony at Rosewood, the reunion with his best friend, his sick Ma. The whole story just came maundering out, and when it was over, he was surprised to see Emma leaning forward in her seat, absorbed. "Wow," she reflected, "Now I see why you look tired. What a day you've had! And how fantastic that we got to skip over all those stupid first date questions and get right into the good stuff."

He laughed, half out of relief, and half out of acknowledgement. She laughed too. *She said 'first date,'* Roy noted. *Does that mean she thinks there'll be a second?* Things were going great, and they hadn't even ordered yet.

"So, what do you want?" Roy asked. "Y'know, the grouper is delicious here, but you gotta try the clams, farmed right here in Cedar Key...heck, I probably grew 'em myself!"

Emma cut him off. "I'm vegetarian. But don't worry, they know me here. There are lots of choices. I've just got to figure out which one I want tonight."

"Y'know, that sounds a lot like life," said Roy.

"What?" Emma looked at him quizzically

"Lots of choices," Roy clarified. "But figuring out which ones are right and which ones are wrong...that's the hard part, y'know? Like messing with that nincompoop Clemson Dawes today. Could've been a bad, bad choice, and it may still be if he ever sees me again, the way he was talkin' threats and trash at me. But if I hadn't made it, something bad might've happened at that ceremony, and I wouldn't have reconnected with Jase. So it was worth the risk. Have you ever made any choices like that? Y'know, risky ones?"

Emma laughed again. He loved her laugh. "Yes, of course! But I rely on something that's been handed down in my family for generations: intuition. We actually all have it. You do too. You followed it in Rosewood. It's just that in my family, we learn how to really trust it, to follow it without question. There's no real rule. It's more of a feeling, and sometimes we get clues from our ancestors."

Now it was Emma's turn to feel sheepish. She normally didn't share these secrets about her relationship with her ancestors with random people, especially those outside of the Tribe. She was surprised that the very intuition she was speaking of didn't stop her from doing so. No, it was okay. Roy needed to hear this. There was a reason.

"Yes, that's it!" Roy concurred. "It was like, even though I knew you were waiting, and I didn't want to be late, I knew I had to stop this jackass-sorry–guy. He was already ruining the ceremony and who knows what else he would've done? But he also saw that I wasn't like him, even though I look like him, kinda. Well, hopefully I'm a little better-lookin.'" He paused and chuckled self-consciously, and then continued. "He needed to see that even though our outside appearances might put us in the same category, we're still different people, y'know? Folks been tellin' me my whole life that I should be this way or that 'cause of how I look an' where I come from, but I don't agree with 'em. 'Specially if it involves other folks gettin' hurt. I guess my pa did me a favor, in a backwards way. When he hurt my Ma and made me lose my best friend, I couldn't see things his way even a little bit, not ever again."

Now this was a conversation Emma could relate to, and she was grateful to Roy for letting his guard so far down. "You're telling me! That's the story of my life, with people expecting me to be a certain way or do certain things or be with certain people just because of how I look."

A third voice boomed, "And mine too!" Both Roy and Emma

jumped in surprise as Jase came barreling over to their table. "Ain't neither one of you two have anything on the black man!" Everyone laughed, and while Roy was happy to see him, he couldn't help but wish he and Emma had just a little more time alone together.

"Jase! Speak of the rat's behind!" Roy bellowed, and the men stood up and gave each other a hug. "Emma, meet Jase, whom you already know about. Jase, this is Emma." Jase and Emma shook hands, and Emma was jolted by an unexpected shock of electricity at their touch. Looking at Jase, she could see that he too was disarmed. His eyes locked briefly with hers, and then quickly darted to the ground. Roy didn't seem to notice as he invited, "Sit down, buddy, sit down! We were just getting ready to order. Ceremony done already?"

"Yea, yea, sorry man, I wanted to give you a little more time since I know you're on a first date and all but..." he paused for a moment when he looked a bit furtively at Emma. "Well, you see Emma, it's just that Roy and I, we haven't seen each other since we were barely men, and I couldn't wait, and forgive me but he didn't let on about how beautiful you were..."

Emma's initial response to Jase cooled immediately. *Oh God, here we go again.* But Roy, having been properly schooled, spoke up on her behalf. "None of that, man! C'mon! Emma isn't here to field old-school smooth operator bull-crap, y'hear? Plus she's MY date, you usurping piece of tunicate!"

"Haha! You remember! Good one!" Jase bellowed.

Emma was interested again. "What? Did you call him a piece of tunicate? You two have an inside joke about *tunicates?* Now, this I gotta hear! The only other people I have ever heard making jokes about tunicates are marine biologists like me, and I know you guys aren't that!"

The three enjoyed food and wine while Roy and Jase

shared story after story of their years growing up on the island together. During those same years, Emma had been growing up in south Florida in a similar way, spending countless days running, climbing, swimming, and playing barefoot in the deep wild places of Big Cypress. Unlike Roy and Jase, however, Emma's childhood never involved violence or fears for her safety. She was with the Tribe until she went off to college. "I can't imagine how hard that must've been," she responded.

As the men continued to reminisce, Emma realized that her date with Roy was morphing into a date between Roy and Jase, who, three beers in and slumped firmly into their seats, looked like they were settling in to talk for hours. She was enjoying the stories, but was also starting to feel like a third wheel. "If you'll excuse me, gentlemen," she interrupted, "I'm going to step out onto the deck for a few minutes and get some air. The full moon is rising."

They acknowledged with hand waves and a couple of nods in her direction as she walked downstairs and out onto the deck at 83 West, which was the lower half of 29 North. It was midsummer, and Cedar Key was free of tourists and snowbirds, so she was by herself. To the east, the rising moonlight was piercing through a pencil drawing of multilayered clouds, creating a silhouette effect that was equal parts spooky and gorgeous. A gentle breeze wafted in from the west, carrying the scents of faraway places. She breathed them in deeply: Mexico, South America, California even. What a world! Right here on this deck, the moon was her reliable companion, and the breeze was her messenger.

With a sudden shift, the wind's tone changed. Coming in from the northeast now, it carried anxiety, trouble, and unrest. She knew these messages...they were the same ones that had blown her way earlier that week on Seahorse Key. Now, however, they were much, much closer. Suddenly, it was clear to her: They were from Cemetery Point Park. They were the swirling vortex of the emotions of lost souls that hadn't been able to find rest in the trees all around them. They were the African American ancestors, too long separated from their roots and branches on account of countless generations spent fleeing, enduring, grieving, and suffering.

Oh, Great Spirit, she thought. *It's so strong here–this grief. How can anyone endure it? What can I do?* Her intuition was clear: she had to go to the cemetery. She didn't know the rest of the plan yet, but she knew that much. Emma ran back upstairs to Roy and Jase. "I have to go now," she said directly. "Something's come up."

Roy looked at his watch, and suddenly became alarmed. "Oh Lord! I gotta go too! Didn't realize time had been gettin' on this much. Gotta get the medicine to my Ma. Jase, man, you ain't driving back tonight, are you? Why not stay on our couch, give us some more time to catch up in the morning?"

"Yea, sure, man, I can do that," Jase responded enthusiastically. He picked up the bill and pulled out his wallet.

Emma pulled out hers as well, ready to pay and exit quickly, but Roy shooed both of their hands away. "It's been a great date, y'know? Like, not what I thought it would be...." he looked over at Emma sheepishly, "....but I haven't smiled this much in many full moons. Thank you both for making me feel like a human again, like I almost have two solid legs to stand on again."

Both Emma and Jase were touched by Roy's words, and Emma found herself still wanting Roy and Jase's company. In fact, her intuition suddenly told her to keep them close by for a little bit longer. "You know, guys, it *is* a full moon tonight, actually, and I was thinking about heading over to Cemetery Point Park. Anyone up for an adventure?"

Knowing nothing of the messages the wind had brought her, both men were surprised at her seemingly impromptu and almost sophomoric-sounding proposal. But the hour was still early, and there was such a sense of ease between them that they agreed. "I live right near the cemetery," replied Roy. "Lemme get the medicines to my Ma, and I can meet y'all out there." Roy paid the bill and they all took leave of the restaurant and headed to their cars.

Alligators

Whether one is talking about the prehistoric creatures or
the denizens of a distinguished university, Florida gators are
perhaps the most famous icon of the state. They are also the
most feared–not only the human versions on the football
field, but also the very real creatures known as the American alligator (*Alligator mississippiensis*). Alligators have been
around for thirty-seven million years, making them true living dinosaurs. Their funny name derives from the moniker
that early Spanish explorers and settlers gave them: *el legarto*
("the lizard"). Growing up to eight hundred pounds in weight
and upwards of fifteen feet in length, these imposing reptiles
are well established as the original top predators of the state.

While they are generally associated with Florida's inland
swamps, springs, and other freshwater ecosystems, alligators
also occasionally find their way to the Cedar Keys' fertile
estuaries. In fact, gator sightings are frequent enough that
the *Cedar Key News* posts regular alligator awareness and
safety tips during the warm mating-season months, when

the reptiles can be especially aggressive.

Just as with sharks, cottonmouths, and other predatory species common to the area, however, unprovoked alligator attacks are extremely rare. The huge population of alligators in the state and their relative proximity to humans, especially with increasing habitat encroachment, is a testament to this fact. Respect is a must for maintenance of this peaceful coexistence: never taunt or feed alligators, don't swim when alligators are clearly present, and never approach a nesting area during mating season.

Go, Gators!

Chapter 13

THE CEMETERY (2022)

SAM WAS BEGINNING to feel like he was nanny to a whole big yardful of spectral toddlers. Every time he wrangled some together, soothed them a bit, and began to see their forms, one would have a tantrum and set the rest of them to fly around inconsolably again. In particular, he was trying to pin down his cousin Floyd, who had been a good friend to him during their living years and could, he hoped, help him with this present endeavor. Unfortunately, while Floyd had a few promising moments of clarity, he proved to be just as susceptible as the rest to the collective unhinging that seemed to grow as each day literally flew by.

Much of Sam's time was spent simply chasing everyone around, like they were engaged in one big game of tag. He tried at first to just sit in one spot and talk everyone into a calmer state of attention, but then he realized that only by behaving like they did–whooshing all over the place–seemed to have any effect. It was during one of those mad whooshings, when he was desperately chasing Cousin Floyd around, that Sam had a revelation. As with all spirits, Sam had gotten accustomed to flying without fear of running into objects, since they simply went right through him. Obstacles like trees, birds, fences, walls, stray cats, and so on were no longer a concern. But, as Sam pursued his erratic cousin through a good-sized cedar tree near Adeline's grave, he was surprised to discover that he didn't come right out the other side. In fact, for a few tranquil moments, the tree totally absorbed him, and he felt both wholly embraced and completely gone. The feeling was at once very familiar to him–it was the feeling he'd had for one hundred years. It was a moment of utter all-rightness, a timeless second of not needing to do or solve anything at all, an instant of abiding peace.

Home.

After a few minutes he was separated from the tree again, back in the midst of uncountable spirits, but the experience inspired him. "So I'm not stuck like this! There's a way to get back to the tree!" Sam actually shouted out loud. The spirits only blubbered some more. *How do I explain this to them, and how can we all rest at last? How do we leave all this woe behind?*

He thought of his granddad and his bedtime stories of the baobab tree in Senegal. One of Sam's favorite legends was the one in which God turned the tree upside down because it was jealous of all the other, more attractive, trees and was unable to feel gratitude for its own life. Now it was even uglier to look at than when it was right side up, but God had also imbued it with healing powers so potent that the tree eventually became an object of worship for humans and animals alike. The tree slowly forgot that it used to feel ugly, and spent the rest of its life working to heal others. The story was a reminder to Sam to be grateful for everything, to emphasize connection instead of the illusion of separation, and to realize that one's value goes far deeper than shallow judgment can comprehend and far wider than a single corporeal form.

So that's it. These souls have been separated for so long that they've forgotten that separation is actually an illusion. I forgot too, when the ceremony started and I learned of the violence and violation of my home. They think they have to hold on to something–like a gravestone–to make their own existence matter.

They've been too long away from their own baobab legends, so
steeped were they in disconnection and bare survival in life, and
now again in death. Here, after generations of severance from
their ancestors, they now cling to the one acknowledgment that
their corporeal time here was real: Adeline Tape's single grave-
stone, the only indication that many African Americans once
lived, worked, thrived and played on this beautiful land.

Sam looked around. The cedar he had just communed with
was rich with green needles and rosewood-colored bark that
stirred his heart. The breeze offered the nourishing smell of
the incoming tide, infused with fresh clean water, and the
herons just beyond the marsh grass at the bottom of the hill
feasted on the bait fish that tumbled in, a twice-daily offering.
Beautiful land! Yes, yes, he saw it, smelled it, felt it, knew it,
and was overcome. The mangroves, the marshes, the cedars,
the oaks, the Spanish moss, the egrets, the fish, the dolphins,
the people. He was so very lucky to have lived, worked, and
played here on these unspoiled grounds and waters. Just as
his grandfather had carried his African homeland with him,
Sam carried this land. In fact, they were but one land: the land
of gratitude, the land of connectedness, the land of *now*. So
sweet, like nectar, was his existence in this land, in life and
in death!

He looked at another red cedar and admired the bark,
which, though dry and cracked in the salty air, was still so
very alive. He drifted into it, and relaxed. *Home.* He emerged
out the other side, and tried his newfound ability on a cabbage
palm. *Home.* Then a live oak, smaller than his own in Rosewood, but still so inviting. *Home!* Oh, how simple! He had to
tell everyone. Everyone!

But how? Even as Sam was learning how to manage his
existence in the spirit realm, his friends and kinfolk seemed to

be dissolving quickly in the other direction. With each passing hour of timeless purgatory, they were becoming blearier and more frazzled, such that they were already near unreachable. Sam felt immense pain bearing witness to their suffering, especially since he knew now: *it simply doesn't have to be.*

They were clinging to a single object—Adeline's gravestone. It was a futile attempt to share the promise of respect and acknowledgment that dear Adeline—who Sam assumed, judging by her absence from the floating masses, was certainly at rest—had been given. They needed more than a remnant stone. They needed to know they were a part of this land, a part of this community, a part of a whole far beyond the tiny plot between two small road signs that read "No Parking: Unmarked Graves."

Sam suddenly realized that he hadn't ever gotten a gravestone either, but somehow his century oak had absorbed him fully nonetheless. Surely, it was because that oak had sustained him and his dad and grandad for three generations. These lost folks needed a reminder that there were trees to merge with everywhere, no farther away from them than right here. But what kind of reminder? Then it came to him: *We may be one with earth and sky, but we also once had bodies and brains and hearts, and we weren't inconsequential. Our connection to this place matters, and acknowledgement of that connection will help those still in corporeal bodies –our descendants–matter too. We need something much more reverential than a modest gravestone churned out by a factory and honoring one lucky individual. We need our own space.*

Sam was grateful for his rapidly evolving insight, but he still didn't know how to put it into action. After all, he was a spirit, and humans couldn't see or hear him even if he could come up with a viable plan. So he did what he usually did when he was at a crossroads: nothing. He rose a little higher to get a view of the whole cemetery beneath him, lit up by the Gulf moon: the peaceful and expansive white section, full of elaborate family plots adorned with both fresh and plastic flowers, and the "Unmarked Graves" section, full of despondency. He saw two war-torn feral cats crumpled together in rough mating, and a possum who wisely ran in the opposite direction. He saw a middle-aged couple walking towards the unmarked graves, one with skin as African black as his own, the other the shade of milk chocolate.

Curious, Sam descended and hovered in front of them, studying their faces. Why were these people in the graveyard in the middle of such a beautiful, moonlit night? Surely, there were more romantic places they could go, especially in Cedar Key.

A cool breeze ruffled Emma's hair and she abruptly stopped walking. She shivered. "Everything okay, Emma?" asked Jase, placing his arm around her. At once, she flushed warm, and the coolness of Sam's presence was neutralized.

"Yes, yes, I think so. It's just that sometimes I get a feeling, an intuition. Don't know what it's about just yet."

"But I thought that was what brought us here?" Jase queried. "Because you sensed something out here you wanted to check out?"

Emma appreciated how seriously he took her reasons for coming to the cemetery. "Yes, that's true," she affirmed, "but this is stronger, more concentrated. And different. The other sensation was of collective despair. There are a whole lot of souls suffering here. But now I feel something else. It's more grounded. Well, I thought I did anyway, but..." She pulled away from the warmth of his arm, and the coolness goose-pimpled her skin again. "Yes, still here. Let's stop walking for a minute, shall we? Roy won't be able to find us if we go too far in. I'd like to hear more about you anyway, Jase: about Rosewood, about your great-grandpa Sam Carter."

Great-grandpa Sam Carter? Sam was taken aback. This handsome man was his great-grandson! He floated even closer to them, listening carefully. He could tell there was a connection between the two of them, and he approved. This woman was beautiful, yes, but from Sam's freshly enlightened viewpoint, she was much more than that. She reminded him of the finest tree, like his own century oak even, rooted and expansive all at the same time. Intuitive. Thoughtful. Wise. And he sensed some kind of connection to her. He could tell Jase did, too. What was it?

Sam listened as Jase recounted the details of Rosewood from his father's—Sam's grandson's—recollection, and Sam was overjoyed to hear that the oral tradition of their homeland had kept the story as accurate and comprehensive as if Sam were telling it himself. Except that Sam didn't know any of the parts that happened after he was lynched on that brutally cold New Year's Day, so he listened raptly and with as much horror as Emma did as Jase unfolded the events that happened in the hours, days, months, and years following the massacre.

It was a hard pill to get down. *Rosewood.* His Rosewood, named after the cedar trees that dotted his beautiful hammock. Built and sustained as a thriving, happy community for many years, and then gone in five days. No real diaspora, just a scattering of survivors and descendants all over the state and country who remained mostly mum about their history. Except for the five people confirmed to have lost their lives in violent succession after Sam, the rest of the scattered community survived through sheer determination, keeping on despite hordes of armed and drunken assailants, subfreezing weather, and with some blessed help from two young Jewish men from up north who whisked survivors away via train. But they were so traumatized that they lived in secret for decades afterwards, afraid to speak of Rosewood lest they be hunted down and lynched themselves. Now, after a century of fear and repressed truth, a decade or so past the death of the last resident of Rosewood, descendants were beginning to speak up, to find each other. They started to educate their communities, and to acknowledge each other and what had happened, with love and connection instead of fear and anger. They were moving forward. And Jase, to Sam's great pride, was one of those people.

The reparations offered by the state were abysmal compared to the loss of land, life, and livelihood, Jase explained. *Can't give 'em too much,* said the good ole boys in Tallahassee, *or else Newberry and Gainesville and Perry and Ocoee and everywhere else there was a lynching in the whole damn state is gonna ask for it too.* Sam felt something warm in his eyes, and saw that Emma was crying. He knew he was feeling her tears as his own, which was as close as a spirit could get to shedding tears. Reflexively, he floated in to hug his great-grandson. He was so very proud of his boy's boy's boy, who was keeping the memory of his family and his people alive. He moved in and encircled his arms around Jase.

Jase suddenly shuddered, stumbled, stiffened, and froze. Emma had to hold his arm to keep him from falling over. "Jase?" She pleaded. "Jase! What's wrong?" *Oh no, is he having a heart attack?*

"Help!" she cried into the warm and buzzing night, hoping maybe Roy was within earshot. But only the cicadas and mosquitoes answered.

Eastern Red Cedar
....

The eponymous tree of the Cedar Keys is the lovely eastern red cedar (*Juniperus virginiana*). As its scientific name suggests, this attractive evergreen is not a cedar at all, but rather a type of juniper, in the same family as redwoods. Its sturdy, attractive bark makes a highly sought-after substitute for true cedarwood; hence the crossover moniker. It is often used as a Christmas tree or as an ornamental native garden tree that is very easy to take care of due to its minimal watering needs and high salt tolerance. Some say that the community of Rosewood was named after the attractive pink bark of the red cedar, which was plentiful in the area at the time.

While a healthy, fully-grown red cedar can reach heights of twenty-five to forty-five feet, almost none of the Cedar Keys' namesake trees are at those heights today. That's because in the early twentieth century they were harvested to near decimation to be cut into pencils that were delivered by the boatload to destinations as far away as England. Thankfully, the trees are slowly repopulating, providing an important

food and nesting source for various species of songbirds and
a great attraction and photo opp for tourists coming to see the
actual "cedars" of the Cedar Keys.

Chapter 14

ATTEMPTED SUICIDE (2022)

THERE WAS ABOUT to be blood everywhere. Roy had seen enough of it in wartime. He saw a lot of it out on the boat too, with regular gashes and scrapes from serrated oysters, brushes against ubiquitous barnacles, and inevitable accidents with filet knives. He never thought he'd see anything close to it in his own living room.

When Roy got home from 29 North/83 West and found his mother on the floor twisting and wailing, he dropped her medicines and his box of leftovers and ran over to her. He grabbed her shoulders and cried, "Ma! Ma! Settle down! Ma! What's the matter? I'm here!" To his horror, he saw that she'd tied a tourniquet around her arm and was holding a paring knife in her white-knuckled hand, an inch above her wrist. "Ma! No! What are you doing?"

"Help me, Roy," she sputtered through the copious tears flowing into her mouth. "I gotta get to 'em. So many of 'em, son. I gotta get to 'em and this is the only way. I gotta enter their world if I'm gonna help 'em. It's up to me now. I've done nothing for so long and can't stand by any longer."

Roy was accustomed to her crying spells and often cryptic way of speaking. She had what folks sometimes called "The Sight," but this wasn't making any sense at all. It was crazy talk. Was she actually trying to kill herself? "Ma! What are you doing? What are you talking about?"

Everyone knew that Roy's Ma had "The Sight," and not just because she told everyone she did. Some of her predictions were eerily accurate, and some were duds, like when she was sure her late husband was going to return to their bedroom and beat the living shit out of her for all of his eternal troubles in Hell. Roy chalked the latter kind of vision up to good old-fashioned PTSD, something he had a great deal of empathy for. As for her other visions, he never questioned her. She predicted her cancer three years before she ever felt the lump in her breast, right down to the day she would detect it. She predicted he would lose a leg in Desert Storm, and she envisioned the lesions on Cedar Key sharks. And, despite her lack of higher education and complete absence of training in meteorology, she was never, ever, wrong about the weather.

Roy still remembers what Ma told him the morning he and Emma met. She said, "Honey, there's a big storm brewin' out there."

Gathering up his snacks in the kitchen for a day of fishing and clamming, Roy looked outside the window at the sunrise. Stars were still twinkling on the sky's ceiling, and the horizon was a paint swirl of yellow and purple. No *red sky in the morning, sailor's warning.* No problem. "Whattaya mean, Ma?" He queried, in spite of her perfect record on weather reporting. "Forecast is clear all day. Looks good out there."

"No, hon, trust me. Big storm. Bad one. But go anyway. You gotta catch a coupla sharks and get 'em checked out by somebody. You gotta go today hon, so please be careful. Big storm brewin' today, and big storm comin' soon after. Not sure I'm gonna make it through."

Roy looked at her sideways as he went out the door, and felt a shudder go through him. "It's gonna be okay, Ma! We're

gonna make it just fine!" Her last statement was uncharacter-
istically morbid. He felt uneasy, and hoped she was wrong
this time.

She was, of course, right about everything.

But at this moment, Roy did not want her to be right. Ma's
eyes caught Roy's in a desperate grip. "Help me cross over, dear
son. I can't reach them any other way."

Roy started sweating. "Reach who? I'm not gonna help you
die, Ma. For god's sake, you're all I got. Who are you tryin' to
reach?"

"The lost souls at the cemetery, Roy. It's been so many years
I've been hearing 'em. I never told you or anybody; they already think I'm crazy enough as it is. But now the souls' cries
are deafening. It's that big storm I been tellin' you about. I can't
take it. I can't do anything about it like this. Your father and
his father and all their pig friends were responsible for this.
For so many years I just stood by, enduring your pa, enabling
him by not doin' anything while I was hearing the sobs from
the cemetery, but I was too afraid to speak up."

She continued, "Remember your best friend ever, Roy? Remember Jase? I could've tried harder to stop your father, but I
was too scared of gettin' beat up. I thought he'd kill me for sure,
and then I wouldn't be there for you, son. I had to protect you
as best as I could. But then your very best friend's father got
beat up instead, and you never saw Jase again. Week in and
week out, and every summer after that, I saw how sad you
were. You never had a friend so good as Jase, ever since. Year
after year I've felt so bad about how your happy childhood
got messed up like that. I am so, so sorry, my son. I was wrong.
I gotta make amends."

For the first time, Roy understood. He understood why
Ma cried all the time, why she treasured and nurtured him

so, why she seemed almost desperate to help people all the time. And then, with relief, he realized how he could stop his mother from her desperate act. "Ma, you're not gonna believe this. Jase is *here!*" His mother, floored, stopped crying almost at once. Roy gently removed the knife from her loosened grasp and undid the tourniquet as he continued, "He's waiting for me at the cemetery now." Ma looked confused. "You remember the date I had tonight? Well, on the way home from Gainesville there was a ceremony at Rosewood, and some jerk tried to mess it up. He was a lot like pa. A real racist pig. And he thought I was like him, you know, and I was afraid too, Ma, really afraid to let him know I wasn't. All them years in the military, standing up to guys twice my size, but someone like this guy still gets to me, makes me feel those old sick fears. But for the first time in my life I confronted one o' those pigs, and it turns out Jase was there, and we stood up to him together and scared him off! Ma, you woulda been so proud. We don't have to stand by any more."

Roy was encouraged by the transformation in his Ma's expression, so he continued. "So Jase crashed my date—I tell ya, if it were anybody else I woulda been mad as hell, but it was Jase! And the three of us have been havin' a time, Ma. My date, Emma, went outside while me and Jase were talkin' and she felt something really strong. She wanted to go to the cemetery—it's like she's got The Sight too—so that's probably why you're feeling this way, why it's so intense. But you can't leave me now, you hear? Ma, we got help now! We're all here together. It's not too late! Pa's story ain't the only one. The story's not over. You don't have to fix this alone."

Ma was quiet as she gathered herself. She stood up, still trembling a little, wiped her face and patted her hair into place. "Son, I want to go to the cemetery now. To the unmarked graves. I want to see Jase." Her voice was calm and clear. Roy nodded, opened the front door and immediately began slapping futilely in response to the itchy welcome of the summer sand gnats, attracted to the nervous sweat on his forehead. Ma didn't seem to notice. She put on her shoes and they walked out the door into the warm and buggy night, mother and son together.

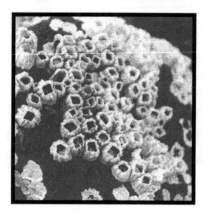

Barnacles

• •

Anyone even remotely familiar with ocean living knows what a barnacle looks like, tries to avoid scraping up against their sharp calcium cones (often called barnacle shells), and tries their best to keep them off of their boats and other floating possessions such as lines, buoys, traps, and the like. Thing is, while most folks may know what a barnacle looks like and how they love to encrust, well, just about everything—from pier pilings to boat hulls to whale's tails— most people do not know what a barnacle actually *is*.

A barnacle is a crustacean, very closely related to crabs, shrimp, and lobsters. If you have the opportunity, place a rock covered in barnacles in a glass jar filled with water. Wait a few moments, and watch carefully. The seemingly lifeless little crusts will open their apertures, and little hairlike cirri will begin to feverishly rake through the water, filtering out food. These efficient little cirri are actually the crustacean's legs, modified specifically for food catching.

Their impressive ability to stick to things so well has to do with a glue they secrete at a fast pace. This glue is so strong and cures so quickly that scientists are researching barnacle secretions for potential commercial applications. Barnacles can stick to anything, from wood to metal to the skin of a manatee. In fact, it's common to spot barnacle imprints on manatees who travel from the Gulf into the Florida springs. Since barnacles cannot survive in fresh water, they die and fall off, leaving circular marks on the manatee's skin.

About seven percent of the world's one thousand species of barnacles live in the Gulf of Mexico. Because barnacles attach to ships, whales, and other objects that can travel great distances, not all of the species are native, and there is concern that non-endemic species may become invasive.

Chapter 15

MERGING (2022)

JASE WAS FAINTLY aware of Emma's strong arms supporting his body as the contours of his insides began to expand
outside the boundaries of his skin. Eventually, he found himself in an infinitely open and peaceful space. The large, blurry
image of a man was moving towards him: he was strong and
muscular, like someone who lifts heavy objects for a living.
As the man grew closer, he could see that the man's arms
were outstretched and inviting, as if expecting a big hug. Jase
shook his head a few times, trying to see more clearly. The
man was materializing even more now. Jase saw broad lips
and high cheekbones that reminded him of his father. But
this man had even darker eyes and bushier eyebrows than
his dad, and Jase suddenly realized who it was. Jase had only
ever seen one grainy old picture of his great-grandpa Sam, set
on the mantle of his parents' home, but the eyebrows were
unmistakable. "Great-grandpa?" he ventured into the closing
space between them.

Sam was overjoyed. He didn't fully understand how this
corporeal/noncorporeal thing worked, but he was open to all
of the gifts being revealed, and this one was the best by far.
"My great-grandson! My great-grandson!"

The two wrapped their arms around each other. Sam buried his face into his great-grandson's shoulder and felt his
heartbeat. *My great-grandson. Alive. Here. With me.*

Jase felt the pliancy of his great-grandfather's not-quite-solid form, but when they pulled back and looked deeply into each other's bright dark eyes, they both started to cry. "Great-grandpa?" queried Jase. "What is happening?"

Sam explained all of it. He told Jase of his last memories in Rosewood, about how much he loved his son, Jase's grandfather, and how proud and relieved he was that they had escaped and carried on. He told him of his century as a tree, his extrication at the very soil ceremony that Jase had attended, his time of deep grief and loneliness in the boat channel, his message from the dolphins, his discovery of the others in the cemetery and his attempts to set them at ease. "Jase, they need acknowledgement. They need recognition. They need assurances that this land and their turn being here is as significant as anyone's. They need to come home, and unless we can calm them down, I can't show them how."

Jase understood. "Great-grandpa, I will make sure this all happens. I'll do my part so you can bring them home."

"Thank you, my great-grandson. I'll meet you at Adeline Tape's grave. Come and see me there whenever you can. I love you. I love you!"

"I love you too!" Jase felt his heart squeeze as Sam pulled away reluctantly.

Emma sat with an immobilized Jase, her mouth agape, propping his muscular build up with the full weight of her own body to keep him from falling over. She dared not slap at the sand gnats, lest Jase fell over. Jase had been speaking the whole time, vocalizing both Sam's and his own words. Her tears welled in gratitude as she understood what was happening.

Roy, approaching from the cemetery entrance with his Ma, could see them in the moonlight: their two bodies were pressed closely together, and as he came closer, he distinctly heard Jase say, "I love you too!" *Well, that was fast, man, and damn forward.* Roy wasn't too sure anymore about how happy he was to see Jase. *I mean, what the hell? First he crashes the date, and now he's professing his love to Emma under the moonlight? I mean, I was only at Ma's for 45 minutes.* He could feel the back of his neck getting prickly and warm.

Ma reached her arm out and touched his shoulder. "Roy, it isn't what you think," she reassured him.

Roy wasn't convinced. "What else could it be, Ma? I mean, look at 'em!"

"Let's get closer," she coaxed. "You'll see."

Emma heard their footsteps as they approached. "Oh Roy, thank goodness you're here!" Roy could see her tear-stained face glistening in the moon's illumination. Her face looked so genuinely compassionate and tender that he could immediately tell they had not been carnally engaged. Plus, he could now vividly see that Jase appeared paralyzed and catatonic. He felt ashamed for having made such a rash assumption. It was his default mode, unfortunately. All his life, starting with his father, Roy had been surrounded by people who never stopped competing with, lying to, cheating on, manipulating, outdoing, out-sexing, and hurting everyone around them. It was no wonder he lived in a fairly constant state of suspicion, guarding against something else he loved getting ripped away.

The curse of the Bamfords, he'd always called it, but now he wasn't so sure. Seemed like maybe the curse could be broken now. He was beginning to see that with his Ma's help, he seemed to have somehow preserved a kernel of wholesomeness at the center of his being, even if his pa never seemed to have had it at all and it sometimes didn't seem like anyone else had it anytime other than Sunday morning, when they all became saints for two hours. He was starting to realize that there might, just might, be others who live in a good way all the time, without ulterior motives or in the service of self-gain. These were the people he wanted to be around, the people he aspired to be like. People like Jase before he was taken away from him, like Helen, who had given him milkshakes to help to allay his grief, like his army brothers before they had all died, like Emma who was clearly involved with a kind of Love much, much bigger than what Roy had mistakenly thought he'd seen when he stepped into the cemetery.

As Roy drew near, Jase suddenly started to stir. "Wh- what? R-Roy? You there?"

Whatever residual concern Roy had about Jase and Emma's romantic status was dispelled when Jase called out for him. He answered, "Hey buddy! Yes! I'm here! And guess what—my Ma is here too! She came to see you! Man, are you all right?"

Ma touched Jase's hand. "Young Jase. It's me, Ma. My, what a tall man you've grown up to be! My heart is so happy to see you. I haven't stopped thinking about you for many years."

Jase was trembling, still recovering from his encounter. He shook his head a few times, adjusting to the moonlight and his surroundings. "Roy. Ma. Emma. No time. Now. We gotta talk." He tried to stand upright, and stumbled. Roy and Emma supported his forearms.

Roy looked to Emma for answers. "I heard him talking, but didn't understand. What was he saying? What just happened?"

Jase jumped in: "The graves. Gotta mark the graves. Gotta calm 'em down, get 'em back home." Both Roy and Ma looked puzzled, so Emma filled in the blanks.

"Jase was just visited by his great-grandfather Sam Carter, of Rosewood." Both Roy and Ma's jaws dropped. Emma explained, "He's here, now, but in the spirit dimension; I can tell because the air is colder here. Sam found a way to connect with Jase. He told him that the suffering here at the cemetery can be alleviated, with our help. We've got to work together, with the community."

"Is that even possible?" asked Roy, overwhelmed. "I mean, it sounds like Jase...talked to a....ghost."

"Not a ghost, son," said Ma. She looked at Emma knowingly. "He talked to his great-grandfather. And now after all them years of being apart, all of us bein' so scared, we can all finally work together. No more fear."

Roy still felt uncertain. He wasn't afraid of spirits. And he loved the fact that all of this meant he would be spending more time with Emma and Jase, and that, after being on the brink of suicide, Ma now seemed to be feeling better than she had in years. But he definitely still feared other ghosts: the ones that wreaked havoc on his past and still seemed to insist on haunting his present, drivers of big red trucks with Bronson Speedway stickers on their windows and plastic testicles hanging off the back. These ghosts hung out at the Scratch Bar and weren't gonna like seeing him hanging around with people who looked like Jase and Emma.

Sam levitated for a moment over the gathering, welling with gratitude as he realized that connections were, at last, restored and well. He vibrated with hope. Soon, after he and Jase laid their kin to rest, he would be in his tree again. He had told Jase he would wait for him at Adeline's grave. So he returned, keeping vigil over the desperate souls, as the party below him walked slowly back to Roy's house.

A breeze blew in from the west, temporarily relieving the influence of sand gnats and mosquitos and carrying a reassurance that Emma, Jase, Roy, and Ma all heard:

Choooooo-kooooooohh.

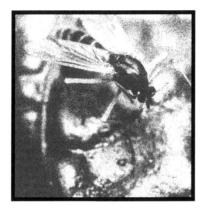

Sand Gnats

Sand gnats, also known as no-see-ums, sand fleas, and bit-ing midges, come out in the warm, humid months and basically torture everybody. They especially like to drive people insane in quiet, breezeless areas around mangroves and salt marshes.

They undoubtedly play an important role in the ecosystem, but this author mainly finds them itchy and maddening.

Chapter 16

CATCHING UP (2022)

"SO, JASE, CAN you stay for a few days?" asked Ma, the relief of finding clarity of purpose making her feel like herself once again. "We could use a proper history professor around here to work with the Historical Society, and we have a mighty comfy couch." She gestured to the oversized Victorian that had been in her family for three generations.

Jase was already planning on it. "Semester doesn't start for a few weeks yet," he replied. "Thanks for the offer! Yes, this is where I need to be for now. We have work to do."

"What about you, Emma?" asked Roy hopefully. "Are you in?" All eyes turned to Emma.

It was late, and Emma knew it was time to take her leave, but she didn't want to go. She was grateful that whatever had happened between all of them this evening was still underway, and she welcomed the energy of a new, meaningful project to work on. She confirmed, "I can shift things around at the lab this week. Count me in. Better be off now, though." She turned to Roy. "Roy, thank you. This has been the most memorable date I've had in a very long time!"

Roy's face turned red. He took that as a cue to walk her out, which Jase supported with a wink and nod. They went out the door, into the brightly soaked wash of the full moon. "Well, that wasn't at all what I had planned for us this evening, but..."

Emma leaned in and kissed him before he could finish his

sentence. He almost fell backwards with the unexpected weight of her body, and then he found her waist in the twilight. He returned the kiss with increasing fervency. Two full minutes later, as their lips parted, Roy flushed and managed to sputter, "Why...what?"

"My intuition," Emma responded matter-of-factly. "See you tomorrow." They shared a final hug, and she walked to her car. Roy watched her get in, start the ignition, and drive off, and then continued gazing down the street for a long, quiet, time. His mind was empty of thoughts, but his heart felt complete.

When he walked back into the living room, Jase and Ma were deep in conversation. Roy didn't have to hear the words in their exchange to know that they were mending their emotional wounds. Somehow, the centuries-old trauma that had assaulted both of their hearts had, on this welcome and unexpected evening, morphed into an outreach of love and understanding between them.

Jase said, "I knew you would have kept him from doing it, if you'd had the power."

"But that's just it, Jase," she lamented. "I've always had the power. I was just too frightened to realize it. Now we gotta make sure other people know they have it, before it's too late."

"Well," Jase replied tenderly, "It isn't too late for us after all, is it?"

"By the grace of God," she replied. They hugged, and Ma went upstairs to bed.

Roy sat down next to Jase on the couch. "Whew, man. It's like in one night we've covered enough ground to make up for the past thirty years!" He slapped Jase on the shoulder.

Jase laughed. "And yet, at the same time, it's like I never left. I mean here we are, two middle aged men..."

"Damn good-lookin' middle aged men...." Roy corrected. He

winked. "I've still got it…"

Jase's eyes widened in recognition. "What, for real! You and Emma, man? That's why you took so long out there? Get it, Roy!"

"Jealous?" Roy queried, only half-jokingly.

"Yes, well obviously," Jase concurred. "But don't worry. It's just like when we were kids on this very same couch, man. If it weren't for your dad and the times, we woulda probably liked the same girls when we were teenagers too. They would've had a hard time choosing between us, the way we look…" Both men high fived, laughing. Jase continued, "But I'm not interested in a girlfriend now, man, not after losing my wife and with everything that just happened. I feel right at home here again, with you. I feel like I'm right where I'm supposed to be."

"Thank God that piss of a dad I had was out fishin' or drinkin' all the time when we were kids. Thank God we didn't both have to deal with his shit in this very house."

"Nope, it was always just us and the insane amount of baked goods your Ma used to feed us in between our outings…. Hell, I'm still working those calories off!" Jase slapped his hint of a paunch. Both men laughed heartily, and then suddenly Roy's face dimmed.

"I just realized," Roy observed, "that I never met your ma or your pa. I never sat on your couch or ate your ma's cookies. I mean, we never talked about it, but we always knew it couldn't ever happen. And I never learned your daddy's secret to catching monster redfish!"

"Well, it's a new day, Roy. You can meet them now, and your daddy ain't gonna whup your ass. They're still in Archer. It's never too late. I mean, after all, I just met my great-grandpa Sam for the first time. But you are NEVER gonna learn my daddy's secret to catching reds, no sir!"

Roy feigned disappointment, and then laughed. "I'll get it from you yet. We'll go fishing again one day soon, and I'll catch you in an unguarded moment..."

"Nah, never gonna happen," mocked Jase. "My daddy said it was a Carter family secret, passed on from his great-great-grandaddy's days as a fisherman in Africa. I'm sworn to secrecy, and now that my great-grandpa Sam can hear me..." he trailed off, shrugging helplessly.

Roy's eyes widened. He was dying to know what actually happened during Jase's mysterious immobilization.

"Jase..." Roy started.

Jase understood. "You wanna know what happened when I met my great-grandpa, don't you?"

"Good time for a beer?" asked Roy, ambling towards the kitchen.

"Love one," replied Jase.

Roy returned from the kitchen with two bottles, and the two men eased back onto the ancient couch. Jase began matter-of-factly with the story of Sam's lynching.

Roy had not been fully prepared for the up-close-and-personal story about Rosewood. I mean, yeah, everyone knew the basic facts—that there had once been a black community there that was wiped out—but the details were never discussed, not in history class, not anywhere. "Sam Carter's watch" was something he heard his pa and his pa's friends say all the time when they were hanging out at the Scratch Bar, like it was the greatest joke in the world. But Roy never knew what it meant. Jase couldn't believe that Roy never knew the whole story, that it wasn't taught anywhere, and that what little Roy did know was so one-sided and vague. Roy hadn't even seen the big Hollywood movie "Rosewood," since he'd been overseas when it came out in theaters. But both men understood why folks around Cedar Key and nearby communities didn't talk about it: the facts were too shameful to say out loud. Many of Roy's lineage were too conscience-stricken to admit their part, whether they'd been directly involved or merely looked the other way. At the same time, he still knew a few of his peers—and the Clem Dawes' of the world—who would do it all over again if the times allowed.

The pit of fear congealed again in Roy's stomach. For the first time, he told Jase about it...how it'd haunted him his whole life, starting with his pa and then right down to earlier that afternoon with Clem Dawes. He said that he felt like Clem was gonna kill him now, no joke.

"That stinks, man," Jase responded. "We gotta watch out for that guy, and believe me, I have practice with this sort of thing." In response to Roy's look of surprise, Jase explained, "Imagine feeling that pit, Roy, not just once in a while, but every damn day of your life. When you go for a jog in a nice neighborhood, or sit down for dinner at a fancy restaurant, even with a bunch of other professors, man, you feel it. Imagine white women looking at you like they're worried you're going to rape them, and store managers hovering nearby to make sure you don't steal anything. No matter that you're a respected, commandment-following deacon of your church and a Ph.D. Emeritus. Imagine what it's like, being a black man in this country."

That pit in his stomach was hard for Roy to handle even once in a while. To live with it on a daily basis like Jase just described? Roy couldn't imagine. But like his Ma, he was starting to understand that he could do something about it.

The Southern Stingray
•••

Down in Tampa Bay, a favorite musical duo, Liz Pennock and Dr. Blues, regularly cranks out a popular local tune called "The Stingray Shuffle." Not only is it a catchy and danceable ditty, it preaches perhaps the most important piece of advice anyone swimming in the warm Gulf waters needs to hear: don't march out into the water. Slide your feet seamlessly from left to right along the sand. This shuffle will allow you to enjoy a refreshing swim without following it up with a trip to the hospital, and save a poor stingray from suffering the indignity and considerable discomfort of being stepped on.

The southern stingray (*Dasyatis americana*) is a docile resident of the warm, shallow, sandy bottom of the Gulf of Mexico. These graceful creatures can range in size from eight inches to several feet across, and have whip-tails that can be longer than their breadth. Because they like to partially bury their bodies in the sand, they can be difficult to spot. While they would not aggressively attack a swimmer, like anyone, stingrays don't like being stepped on. In such an unfortunate case, the aptly named whip-tail reflexively flips up, embedding a poisonous and extremely painful stinger in the hapless beachgoer's lower leg. Contrary to popular belief, one cannot relieve the pain or mitigate the venom of a ray's sting by peeing on the wound. Best bet if you have the misfortune of being stung? Pour hot (not boiling) water and salt into the wound, remove any traces of the barb from the area, and get right to the hospital. Thankfully, unlike with some other species of stingrays, the sting of *Dasyatis* is painful but rarely lethal.

Unlike their clam-crazy cousin the cownose ray, southern stingrays do not form massive schools. And while they might enjoy a tasty bivalve or three as part of their varied diet of crustaceans, worms, and small fish, they are not much of a threat to the Cedar Keys' clam farm industry.

Chapter 17

THE SCRATCH BAR (2022)

EMMA ANSWERED HER phone first thing the next morning. "Hello?"

"Emma, it's me, Jase. Wondering if you'd like to accompany me to the Cedar Key Historical Society at three o'clock this afternoon? I made an appointment with the director Anna Hodges, and it would be great to have you there to share your background and interest in restoring the unmarked gravesites."

Emma would have just enough time to get to the lab to check and feed her specimens and make it back to the main island by three o'clock. "Yes, count me in. Is Roy meeting us there?"

"He can't. Something about how his clams need checking and the tides are optimal right at that time. But he said he'd meet up with us later."

Emma paused, suddenly feeling self-conscious. It was just a meeting, not a date. She'd already stepped way out of her comfort zone last night, when she'd impetuously kissed Roy. She'd regretted it almost immediately, intuition or not, realizing that the whole thing was going to distract from the project they were all embarking on together. To complicate matters, she also felt a whiff of connection to Jase, and she didn't want any of it. She needed more time. She did not want or need any of this hormonal bother, this ancient chemistry churning inside of her, intent on propagating the species via the nectar of attraction.

Unlike with past relationships, however, these two men had become energetically intimate with her within the span of twenty-four whirlwind hours. They had shared an experience that few have ever known, even among the most intuitive and connected members of her own Tribe. They were on an important path together, and she knew well that any naturally unfolding path must be kept free of obstacles. She had to keep it all platonic, if only to stay open to the signs from the ancestors that would reveal the path forward. She remembered how the warmth of Jase's arm around her had canceled out her ability to sense Sam. She knew that the signs were beginning to assert themselves with increasing frequency all around her, but she also knew she could become deaf to them if she lost her focus.

She gave Jase a curt response: "OK. Meet you there. Thanks!"

A few minutes before three o'clock, Emma walked up to the Cedar Key Historical Society and Museum where State Road 24 intersected 2nd Street. The scene was busy that beautiful autumn afternoon, with beer and ice trucks pouring in to stock the various eateries and bars for the weekend and pods of loud bikers cruising in from all parts of the state for some friendly Gulf-side carousing. Locals rotated in and out of the post office and the Market grocery store, grabbing chips and sodas before heading out on the water. Tropically-clothed, straw-hatted tourists chatted on the charming street corners nearby, nursing lattes and stuffed bagels from the 1842 Grind and Mercantile and homemade acai bowls and smoothies from the pink Prickly Palm cafe across the street. Fat, not-very-stray cats breezed between their legs, glamouring vulnerable newcomers into giving them scraps of gluten-free quiche or stuffed everything bagels.

Golf carts dotted the parking areas up and down 2nd all the way to City Park. There was a big cluster of them by the Cedar Keyhole Co-Op Art Gallery, where they were preparing for an indoor/outdoor weekend opening. Artists spilled into the sidewalk, setting up easels, tables and tents just outside, arranging their works. Just a little further down, another clutch of golf carts up at the Community Garden spoke to the perfect weather, as several folks had gathered to tend to their fall plantings. Emma could hear occasional bursts of laughter from the two gatherings, and the happy sense of group purpose and activity made her smile.

Emma spotted Jase waiting for her next to a small eastern red cedar tree across the street from the museum. He looked dashing, dressed in a gray blazer over a black shirt with matching gray pants and black dress shoes. It was such an uncommon look for the island, where most folks wore socks and sandals or clam boots in the winter and flip-flops in the summer, even when paired with their best Sunday threads. He grinned wide when he saw her. "Well, good afternoon…!" He resisted the temptation to add "…beautiful," understanding that it would sound like a platitude. But she sure was, just like she had been last night, just like she surely must always be. *No wonder Roy asked her out. Damn.*

Their hands met for a formal shake, and there it was again: that jolt of energy that passed right through her, and the barely perceptible tick in Jase's face that indicated that she wasn't alone. Seems there was no way they would be able to evade the ancient alchemy of attraction, but they could get beyond it. She was sure of that.

The meeting with the director of the museum went well. It seemed that while most folks couldn't consciously hear and feel the agony of the many afflicted souls, more subtle forces were at work. Just that week, Emma and Jase learned the museum had applied for a grant to work with an archeologist named Dr. Edward Gonzalez-Tennant from University of Central Florida to take imaging of the area and find the specific locations of the as-yet-unknown number of unmarked graves and to uncover, document, and memorialize the identities of those who might be buried there. They had begun an investigation to find out more about Adeline Tape, and had already devised a historical walking tour of the Hill and the cemetery, emphasizing the prevalence and importance of African Americans to the area's history. Best of all, after decades of most people not even knowing about the real, unbiased story of Rosewood or the once vibrant African American population in Cedar Key, the museum was preparing at long last to unveil a permanent African American history exhibit.

Some not-so-subtle forces were hard at work too, like the pistol of a matriarchal Rosewood descendant who presented at the Historical Society every couple of months or so demanding public acknowledgment and education, and the elegant, espresso-skinned grandmother from Chiefland who created Cedar Key paintings and lovingly compiled photos depicting the African American history of Levy County into books that the Historical Society displayed and sold. Folks who had lived in the area for generations were beginning to inquire with genuine interest about the "novelty" of African Americans who resided here in the past, and newcomers visiting the Historical Society openly inquired about why the community wasn't more diverse today.

In fact, the lack of African Americans on the Nature Coast of Florida is a relatively recent phenomenon, driven by the tragedy of the Jim Crow era, also known as the "lynching

decades." Cedar Key became infamously known in the mid-
to late twentieth century as one of the "Sundown Towns,"
meaning that descendants or supporters attempting to visit
Rosewood or lay flowers on one of the cemetery headstones
would get verbally threatened or even shot at, and anyone
with black or brown skin would be made to feel very unwelcome after sunset. For some older residents raised in the
shadow of Jim Crow, it still felt like this. But with the turn
of the most recent century, while endemic fishermen were
training for a new future in clamming, an influx of artists,
writers, yogis, scientists, and professors pulled Cedar Key into
a new era of thought and attitude. These new transplants—
though still mostly white—were not racists, at least not in
principle. Some came down only for the winter months and
were known as "snowbirds," while others settled year-round,
transforming every few home fronts into artists' sculpture
gardens or pastel-painted AirBnb's.

The inelegant error of some of the new folks, however, was
that they set themselves apart from the fourth-, fifth-, and
sixth-generation islanders, and some of the longtime locals
did the same thing in turn. They created less-than-compli-
mentary names for each other, and regarded each other with
a mostly unspoken judgment that occasionally manifested in
neighbors trying to outdo each other with bigger and bigger
flags touting opposing political parties. On the surface, the
town was beginning to show signs of divisiveness, but the
deeper truth was that everyone was too smitten with the
island for it to ever become a real issue. As the years went
on, sixth-generation locals became award-winning artists,
retired professors became profitable clammers, and everyone
always showed up and cheered during the Christmas lighting
festivities the day after Thanksgiving.

So most everyone in town was likely to be receptive, and even openly appreciative, of the Cedar Key Historical Society's African American exhibit and cemetery project. Almost everyone, that is, except for the small but volatile posse of regulars at the Scratch Bar, the last vestige of a time when it was viscerally dangerous simply to live while black or brown in these parts.

The Scratch Bar was on State Road 24, closer to the mainland than to the main island, tucked back between an oyster house and a boat-storage building in front of a stand of small, scraggly cedar trees. Some of the neon letters in "Scratch" had blown out years ago, making the sign look like it said "rat Bar." No one seemed to object. It was there that Clemson Dawes hung out every weekend after fishing, before hightailing it back to Bronson under the influence. This afternoon, while Emma and Jase were engaged in a heartening discussion at the Historical Society, Clem was getting especially inebriated. Once his lips were good and loose, he launched a raging diatribe to an appreciative audience of four other drunks.

"Fucking blacks out at Rosewood," he started, pausing so his barmates had time to shake their heads in commiseration. "Big-ass group of em, all dressed up like they was doin' somethin' oh so fucking important." More tsk tsks, more shaking heads. "Some nerve they got, trespassin' on land wasn't never even theirs in the first fucking place, no matter what they say. They was lucky to be at Rosewood. Lucky to have jobs and not be owned. Just had to go an' mess it up, feeling their oats, messin' with a white woman."

"Damn straight," agreed one of the pickled heads at the bar. "So what'd you do, Clem?"

"Did what I had to, man. I put 'em in their place. I tol' 'em to go the fuck home and quit their trespassin'. I parked and got outta my truck and went up to 'em!"

"YEA!" hooted a man with a big belly and a grizzly beard. "Kick 'em around some!"

"Remind 'em they ain't welcome here!" another hollered enthusiastically.

But now Clem was going in for the kill. "Well, I actually thought that might happen, see, because another white dude pulled up next to me in his pickup, started walkin' with me, an' I gave him the salute."

Someone cheered, "That's what you needed, man! Reinforcements! Yea!"

Clem shook his reddening head, and the vein between his eyes began to bulge. "Not so fast. He was a fucking traitor, man. Came walkin' next to me all like he owned the place. A pussy fuckin' turncoat. He was friends with one of the blacks, and they both got all fat-chested and told me to leave. Hell, maybe that white sonofabitch was a rainbow bastard, protecting his darkie boyfriend, for all I know."

Someone shouted, "Shit, Clem! A twofer! Did you kick their asses?"

"Hell no! Weren't worth my time with all them colored witnesses just staring at me all offended and high and mighty and whatnot, so I left. But hear me, boys: they ain't seen the last of my face or my fist. Especially that fucking rainbow turncoat—Roy, he said his name was."

The four men looked up simultaneously. "Roy Bamford?" said the eldest drunk, tentatively.

Clem brightened. "You know the fucker?"

"Hell, yea!" The elder man nodded. "Damn good fisherman and clammer, and his dad, Roy the Second, and his grandad, Roy the First, were the kings of the Scratch Bar. Real grand wizards of our chapter, if you know what I mean. His daddy was a good friend of mine. We used to tear up this town, keep it safe from unwelcome influences, y'know?"

"What happened to his daddy?" asked Clem.

"Sad story. He just up an' died when he was out shark fishin' one day. He was barely forty. I miss the bastard. But I always thought ol' Roy the Third was a good guy, anyway. They say he's a war hero. Keeps to himself these days. Takes care of his Ma. Thought he was still one of us at heart. Apparently, I don't know shit."

Clem's blue eyes squinted. "Well, we'll avenge ol' Roy the-sack-of-shit Third's daddy then, next time I see that traitor. According to ol' Sam Carter's watch, that time is comin' real soon. War hero, my ass."

Almost everyone in the chapter cheered except for the big-bellied guy, who was puking into his beer stein.

Cabbage Palms

The hearts of palm salad is one of Cedar Keys most unique and iconic culinary offerings. When tourists first try the crunchy, nutty strips of the heart of the palm, the question inevitably arises: Did they have to kill the palm tree to get the heart out?

Well, yes. It can be a controversial topic, as palm trees are one of Florida's most treasured symbols. Most species of palms in Florida—both native and non-native—have a "heart," which is actually the tender and very edible core of the tree. To harvest it, you have to cut the tree down and chop the core into pieces. For this reason, it is not a good idea to retrieve hearts of palm from the less-abundant, long-lived species.

Enter the cabbage palm (*Sabal palmetto*). Unlike its tall supermodel cousin the coconut palm, which keeps itself exclusively to the southern part of Florida, native cabbage palms are a bit stockier, much more cold hardy, and grow all over the state in a whole variety of conditions. They have the honor of being the state tree, probably because of their sheer abundance. Like coconut palms, cabbage palms do have very long life spans; yet they are so common that folks consider them weeds in some areas, and smaller ones are often thinned out in Florida panther habitats just to make it easier for the big cats to roam.

Seminole Indians used the cabbage palms for the construction of chickees and other buildings, drying racks, and for their delicious hearts, which also happen to be very nutritious.

So copious and available are cabbage palms that their hearts have come to be known as "swamp cabbage." If you want to try it, just make sure you are cutting down a single tree from a site densely populated with cabbage palms versus from an area in which someone is using them for landscaping. Better yet, go to one of the state's swamp cabbage festivals, or contact the Florida Forest Service to find out where cabbage palms are already being thinned out. Or avoid any hard labor altogether and go to a restaurant in Cedar Key to enjoy a delicious hearts of palm salad.

Chapter 18

PALM SALADS (2022)

AFTER THE MEETING with the Cedar Key Historical Society, Jase gave Roy a call. Roy was still on the water, so Jase
suggested that he and Emma have some coffee and a bite to eat
at the Island Hotel while they waited for him. Emma agreed.
She hadn't been there for years, opting instead to cook and
eat by herself at the lighthouse, have a vegetarian special at
29 North, or hit some of the more local hangouts like Annie's
or 2nd Street Cafe.

The Island Hotel was a famous tourist destination with a
rich and scandalous history replete with murders, whores,
hauntings, and a whole host of famous patrons including
President Grover Cleveland, John Muir, Pearl S. Buck, and
Jimmy Buffett. The most recent famous person to visit had
been the charismatic Chief James E. Billie, former chairman
of the Seminole Tribe, who had taken it upon himself to visit
Emma with his family. That was the last time she had been
there. The hotel had survived the Civil War, the Seminole
Wars, the hurricanes of 1896, 1935, and 1950, and every hurricane since. Water stains still marked the Neptune mural in
the hotel bar from seepage after Hurricane Easy's not so easy
assault on the island in 1950.

Emma and Jase each ordered the famous hearts of palm
salad and were presented with a giant bed of greens garnished
with the raw heart of a cabbage palm, dates, seasonal fruits
like strawberries and peaches, and topped off with a generous

scoop of green peanut butter ice cream made with vanilla ice cream, peanut butter, mayonnaise, and green food coloring. As shocking as it sounds, the flavors somehow meld into an exquisite gustatory experience, and tourists came from hundreds of miles away to enjoy the iconic delicacy.

"You know this palm salad was invented by the owner of the Island Hotel in the 1940's?" Emma offered casually.

"See, that's only partly true," Jase corrected. "My momma was actually a third cousin to the head cook, Catherine 'Big Buster' Johnson. Bessie Gibbs, the owner of the hotel at the time, loved to cook, and she admired Big Buster's unique recipes. It was actually Big Buster who invented the palm salad, and Ms. Gibbs who brought it to the spotlight. The palm salad is a Cedar Key icon, and it was invented by an African American. But see? Folks don't know that."

Emma nodded sympathetically. "At least the Historical Society is doing something about it."

Jase nodded in return, but his tone was worried. "Yes. But we've gotta move even faster than the Historical Society on the cemetery, Emma. My great-grandpa Sam didn't think the ancestors have a whole lotta time before their misery becomes permanent."

Emma nodded again gravely. They had opted not to tell the Historical Society's director about either of their spirit encounters, neither Emma's intuitive ability to gauge the source and cause of the unsettled energy coming from the section of the cemetery that contained the unmarked graves, or Jase's direct merging with his long-dead great-grandfather. Most folks would think it a bit "off" at best, and some more fervent types might even declare it to be the work of Satan. As academicians, both Jase and Emma also understood that the historians and archeologists needed to work with facts, not phantom stories. So, how to speed the process along?

After a moment's pause while they both pondered their options, Jase took a breath and announced, "I'm gonna have to front the money for the cemetery markers myself."

Emma looked perturbed. "We're talking a few thousand dollars here, Jase, what for proper signage, research, a website, more?"

Jase shook his head. "We don't even need to do that much just now. That'll all come. And I can write for a few grants of my own, and get reimbursed. Right now we need to do just enough to get the spirits to settle down a little so Great-grandpa Sam can teach them about the trees."

Emma concurred appreciatively as she said, "Yes. Yes. The trees."

Jase was curious. Emma's heart was clearly deeply invested in this history and this project. "I don't get it, Emma. I mean, I'm African American and a history professor, and a direct descendant of folks who lived in these parts. So it makes sense that I'm advocating for this project. You're a biologist, and a Native American. Why this interest in helping my people?"

Emma looked bemused. She never did fully understand why people, even smart, well-meaning, equality-oriented people, still liked to compartmentalize themselves so. "Sure, Jase, we have the labels and the DNA that say you're African American and I'm Native American, that you're a historian and I'm a biologist, that you're a man and I'm a woman...." She watched as that last comparison made him shift noticeably in his seat. "But look closer. My ancestors, who lived here long before Africans and Europeans, taught me that we all come from the same firmament, expressing ourselves in myriad ways as the Universe freely turns. We may look different or have different stories, but we are all functioning from the same source. So your people are my people, and my people are your people."

Jase was transfixed as she continued, "Remember the story about the baobab tree you told me? And your great-grandpa's discovery about how he was a tree, and he can show all the spirits how to be too? That is the same for 'my people.' We all return to the firmament; heck, we never left. Out at the Cedar Key Shell Mound, the ancients had burial sites just like people do today. They faced the setting sun, which my people believed to be the entryway to the underworld. That setting sun rises again, day after day, and the cycle of life and death continues, and we are all intimately part of that. But so many people get so far removed from ever seeing that, Jase. Some, like too many African Americans, were forcibly extricated from a life that didn't differentiate between earth and sky. Others, like so many in modern culture, let greed, materialism, ego and anger build barriers that wall themselves off from the great wide heaven."

Jase, though thoroughly entranced and even recognizing principles from his own faith, still harbored doubt. "How do your ancestors teach you? They're dead. And why did Sam become a tree, while all of these other folks are still lost and detached?"

Emma considered it for a moment, then said, "My ancestors taught me in the same way that Sam taught you. We have a rich oral history as well, which, just like your knowledge from your great-grandpa's grandpa, gets passed down almost perfectly intact generation after generation. But we also have a connection to the trees, which long after bodies go into the ground, hold our ancestors as One. Because of Sam's grandpa being from Africa, I think, and the daily good life Sam shared with that oak tree in the community of Rosewood, he just naturally became the tree when he was released from his corporeal self. Until his violent murder, he never knew the suffering of so many in the Jim Crow era until the very end. And that's why he remained as a tree for one hundred years, until the soil ceremony. He finally felt it when the soil was moved and the horrors were acknowledged out loud."

Jase asked, "Okay, so I get that you see the connections between us. I feel that too. But still—this isn't your academic work or your research, yet you're as interested in it as if it were. Why?"

Emma became serious as she looked right into Jase's clear black eyes. "My work, my science, is all about the greater reality of connectivity and balance. The planet is changing very quickly because she is dangerously out of balance. Seas are rising faster than we realized, pollution is rampant, and humans declare war on each other and the whole planet in small, large, and cataclysmic ways. My academic work—examining various species, testing the water and correlating the water qualities to the health of the species—is much like listening to the wind and hearing that something is wrong. When there is dis-ease, my responsibility is to try, in any way I can, to restore balance, health, and harmony. At this level, once again, it is all part of the same wide sphere. The oceans, the land, the animals, the people, the living, the dead—all one. Stewardship of the land and of each other are one continuous charge. Your people and my people both have a long history of honoring this commitment. In fact, your people found refuge with my Tribe during slavery days. The Black Seminoles."

Her words wrapped around Jase like a tender ballad. Of course. Of course. They were totally connected. "Don't I know it!" Jase acknowledged. "My great-great-grandmother, Altamese Burgess, was a Black Seminole."

Emma's eyes grew wide with surprise. "What?! That's my great-great-grandmother's name on my father's side," she said breathlessly. "Could it be? Jase, we're fourth cousins!"

Impulsively, they reached out to take each other's hands. So that was the attraction, the electricity of recognition between them. They were kin.

After securing his boat and washing up quickly, Roy rushed into the dining room just in time to witness the tender moment. He bowed his head, realizing that Jase had spent more one-on-one time with Emma during their "meeting" than he ever got to on his first and apparently only date. Fine. NO problem. He didn't want any beef with his rediscovered best friend, and he was beginning to feel as if both Jase and Emma were way out of his league anyway. After all, he'd never left this town other than during wartime, never gone to college. They, on the other hand, were perfect for each other. He turned for the exit as inconspicuously as he could, but not before Jase spotted him.

"Roy! Buddy!" boomed Jase's voice. "We're over here, man!"

Roy spun self-consciously around, half expecting to see their hands still entwined, but Emma was pulling over another chair as she waved him over. "Lots to talk about!" She beckoned. "Have a seat!"

As soon as he sat down, he felt an ease restored between them. "What'd I miss?" asked Roy, feeling both eager to catch up and uncertain about what he'd just witnessed.

They leaned in close. Emma could smell the mint on Roy's breath, no doubt popped a few moments beforehand in anticipation of being close to her. Roy, meanwhile, smelled Jase's musky cologne wafting up from the open chest buttons of his shirt, suddenly self-conscious that he himself probably smelled like eau de fish entrails, wondering if Jase was trying to make himself alluring for Emma. Emma noticed the uncertainty right away, and dispelled it in one sentence: "Roy, guess what? Jase and I just discovered that we're related to each other. We're cousins. We have the same great-great-grandmother!"

Roy could not hide his relief. "Oh, oh wow. Oh, that's great!" Whether he and Emma were ever going to be more than friends or not, he was beginning to loathe liking them both so much, knowing that he could lose one or both of them to the entanglements of attraction and jealousy despite their best efforts. With Jase's reappearance into his life, he was beginning to understand his decades of loneliness: his only genuine friends since Jase went away were his unit brothers, and they had all died. In the years since returning home, he'd reckoned with the wounds of his upbringing by keeping to himself, away from the influences that wanted to pull him away from who he really wanted to be. Now, here in front of him were two good friends at last, one old and one new, and he didn't feel so alone. And they were cousins. *Cousins! Thank the Almighty.*

Emma laughed, easily reading his sense of relief, and feeling it herself. She continued to catch Roy up. "So the meeting with the Historical Society went really well, and they are happy we can work with them," she began. "Jase is going to front some money to put up signs at the unmarked gravesites. He can write for grants in partnership with the Historical Society and get reimbursed later. We are going to have a dedication at the site, and Jase will read out the names of those he believes might be buried there, based on the death records. He'll also read the names of those who died in Rosewood. I'm going to lead a fire ceremony, as an invitation for everyone to honor the deceased. At that point, hopefully, the spirits will be appeased and Jase's great-grandfather will be able to reach them and teach them how to finally be at rest. I'll know by the quality of the breeze." She felt grateful that she could speak to them straightforwardly using words that most would consider somewhat "woo" or even downright possessed. "Of course," she winked, "we can't tell people that last part."

Jase nodded enthusiastically, but Roy looked thoughtful. "What about Rosewood?"

"Rosewood?" Jase asked with surprise.

Roy nodded. "I never knew what really happened, not 'till you felt like it was safe enough to tell me, after all these years. You said your great-grandpa had family in Cedar Key, but isn't there a graveyard in Rosewood too? What about the five or more other folks that died there, like your great-grandpa? What about the relatives and friends here who knew them? Shouldn't we honor them too? Shouldn't everybody know about it?"

Jase became solemn. "Great-grandpa Sam said he never heard anyone wailing from Rosewood. He called out for a long time, but no one answered. He said the ones that didn't find their rest came here, to Cemetery Point Park. He said his cousin Floyd told him that some of the Rosewood folks came out here too, like he did, trying to find someone, anyone, but he can't reach any of them. Sam seems very intent on finishing his work here before going back home to rest. Besides, Rosewood cemetery is on private property now. We can't get to it."

Roy wasn't deterred. "Unless...we get permission. Like you did for the soil ceremony."

Jase couldn't deny the irony. "Permission to go to our own families' cemetery. No matter how much time goes by, I can't get over it; it's just so unfair. You know, in Atlanta they built an exit right through an African American cemetery. Right off I-75. You can see the headstones as you come off the off-ramp. The indignity of all of it really burns."

Emma chimed in, "All the more reason, cousin!" Jase and Roy both brightened with the reminder of the newly discovered family relationship. "The Historical Society said they worked with the archeologist from University of Central Florida who got access to the cemetery. And you know the owners. They seemed reasonable, right?" Jase nodded. "They'll help."

Jase thought for a moment, and then his eyes brightened. "A Rosewood reunion! We have them every year, all of us descendants, all over the state. But this year, exactly one hundred years after Rosewood was burned down, we should have it here. My great aunt Altamese Wrispus is the director of the reunion board. I'll propose it to her. We can start here at the Cedar Key cemetery, then go to the Rosewood family plots after we get permission. Everyone can stay here in Cedar Key, have a barbecue at the beach park. It'll be special. Y'all got any plans for New Year's?"

Emma and Roy smiled. "We do now," they responded in unison.

Horseshoe Crabs

A casual glance into the waters along the Cedar Key shore-line during spring and autumn months will reveal a large number of unusual invertebrates called horseshoe crabs (*Limulus polyphemus*), especially during new and full moons. Horseshoe crabs are not really crabs at all, but prehistoric arachnids. Having been around for hundreds of millions of years, they are among the oldest surviving species on earth, and are often referred to as living fossils.

The carapace of a horseshoe crab is helmet-shaped and can range in size from an inch to a foot in diameter. They have a protruding tail called a telson that extends a few inches and can, from the top view, make the animal resemble a small stingray at first glance. From the bottom up, the arthropod reveals its crab-like features, with six rows of legs and five sets of claws. Despite its imposing appearance, however, horseshoe crabs are harmless.

These animals have showy biannual mating rituals, con-gregating in mating clumps of several animals at a time in order to achieve the most fertile outcome. The resulting eggs are a very important source of food for several species of seabirds. A vibrant horseshoe crab population thus ensures that seabird populations also remain healthy. These gentle creatures have been supporting the web of life for a very long time.

More recently, science has revealed a direct link between horseshoe crabs and human health. They have a unique compound in their blood, Limulus amebocyte lysate, that is used to test for the safety of all vaccines administered in the United States.

Horseshoe crabs live an unusually long time compared to most invertebrates, and don't reach sexual maturity for at least ten years. It is for this reason, in conjunction with their gentle, slow-moving nature, easy accessibility from shore, and importance to human health and ecology that the University of Florida has created an extensive citizen science program called Florida Horseshoe Crab Watch to monitor the populations of these vulnerable and important creatures.

Chapter 19

RED TIDE (2022)

AUTUMN TAUNTED THE residents of Cedar Key with occasional cool days and tiny bits of color dusting the sweet-gum trees and southern red maples nestled amidst a buffet of evergreen cedars, oaks, palmettos, and palm trees. It was the busiest season for clamming, and Roy spent long hours on his bird dog on each of his seven two-acre tracts laying seed clams, transferring the grow-outs to bigger net bags, and doing lots of harvesting on his mature beds. He was working faster and harder than usual. Red tide had been lurking to the south, but was now seeping its way up the Florida west coast and had smothered the waters just north of Dog Island, ruining the holidays for the clammers who leased farm beds there. Those clammers like Roy who were lucky enough to rent underwater farmland south of the island were work-ing double time to make sure they grew and harvested their clams at maximum productivity in case the tendrils of red tide licked them all out of commission. Clamming may be a whole different skill than the grouper fishing he and his pa used to do, but it was still much the same life economically: feast or famine, depending on God's mood.

Clamming, fishing, and farming all depended on the mercy of Mother Nature, and lately Mother Nature was increasingly at the mercy of *Homo sapiens'* poor choices. It wasn't even grist for a spirited debate over morning coffee any more, just a somber and mostly unspoken recognition: the climate was changing quickly.

The tiny little red tide dinoflagellate, *Karenia brevis,* is naturally occurring in warmer southeastern waters, occasionally blooming and suffocating small sections of the ocean in much the same way a lightning strike occasionally hits and stresses out parts of a forest. But unlike the understory-culling benefits of natural burns, red tide has no known direct ecological benefit. Like the devastating wildfires that burn out of control, red tide causes mass destruction if its blooms become abnormally far-reaching. Lately red tide was displaying an efflorescence beyond the occasional tragic-but-temporary fish-killing, eye-watering local event. "Dead zones" of the harmful algae and their aftermath had started mapping whole sections of the Gulf of Mexico, and the ecological and economic results were devastatingly long lived.

Roy had recently been wondering how long it was going to take the harmful algae to reach these pristine waters. He looked out over the wide, undeveloped shorelines of Cedar Point and Lagos Key, marveling with satisfaction at how they had remained condo- and mansion-free. This near miracle was due, in part, to the successful lobbying of the Cedar Key Aquaculture Association, which he helped found, to have the Cedar Key Refuge boundaries expanded to include these critical shorelines. *It helps the clams, it helps the clammers, it helps the businesses who buy from the clammers, it helps the animals who come to the artificial reefs made by the clam farms; I mean, if you keep connecting the dots, it helps the whole planet,* Roy thought. *And then comes this algae from hell—not once or twice every few years like normal, but twice a year, maybe more—and in some places it doesn't ever go away. It just moves around, killing our fish and clams, not to mention our livelihoods. I finally got to where I've learned, and even like, this job. But how long will I have it for?*

His thoughts turned to pleading. *God, I ain't been to church in a long time. In fact, and please hear me out here, Lord: it's not 'cause I'm not a spiritual man. It's just that your creations—this ocean and these islands—are way more sacred to me than some fancy white building with stained glass windows that I gotta get all dressed up to go into. I ain't a prayin' man 'cause you already give us everything we could possibly need. We're supposed to be able to figure the rest out for ourselves with the brains you gave us. But we're not treating your gifts right, God. So if you don't mind, I'll do just one prayer right here: please help everyone see that we're fuckin' messin' it all up. Oops, sorry 'bout that, God. I'm just so damn frustrated. Oops, sorry again. I'm trying to do my part, Lord, but I'm feelin' small. I can't fight these big-money, big-power folks. We may have kept the high-rise buildings and golf courses away from here, but we're still getting the effects of everything they're doin' everywhere else. Please, Lord, help them see.*

The more self-serving politicians and dollar sign opportunists called it a "natural phenomenon," but Roy and every other clammer and oysterman—laboring in the Gulf day in and day out—knew better. The mega-blooms followed the nutrients, and Florida was drowning in nutrients from fertilizer runoff. Meanwhile, herbicides utilized in equally plentiful amounts were killing off the good algae and pesky aquatic plants that uninformed waterfront homeowners didn't like. Not only did that good algae keep Roy's clams happy and those "pesky" water hyacinths serve as a favored snack for the soon-to-be-starving manatees, they both helped to keep the red tide in check. Yep. They were being killed off to pad the pocketbooks of the companies that continued to promote Florida's decidedly unsustainable golf-course aesthetic. These same companies donated millions to support the types of politicians that would let them just keep on doing it. When waterfront homeowners rubbed their red-tide-stung eyes and held their noses in response to the wicked stench of all the dead fish piling up along their seawalls, they were told it was a "natural phenomenon." *Oh, the politicians and fertilizer companies may be rolling in the play-dough now,* Roy thought grimly, *but if the cycle continues for even a little bit longer, the only ones who are going to end up with long-term profit are the dinoflagellates.*

So Roy breathed in the still-refreshing, toxin-free air and marveled that his tiny corner of this development-ridden state was still, at least for now, hanging on. He admired the healthy manatees munching on the succulent *Thalassia* and *Syringodium* seagrasses that blanketed the shallow bottoms on his way in and out from his clam farms, and the clusters of prehistoric *Limulus* horseshoe crabs engaging in their group mating dance. He started to consider what he would do if it all went to hell, like it seemed to be doing everywhere else. He remembered hearing something about Manatee Springs being overtaken by algae, just like what happened in the Indian River Lagoon on Florida's east coast right before all the manatees started dying of malnutrition and starvation. But he hadn't been there in years, and the manatees in the shallows of the Cedar Keys didn't look any the worse for wear. If it weren't for the occasional mentions from his colleagues, he wouldn't have known anything was going sour. So today, he would work hard at his sustainable organic clam farm, knowing that he was helping to at least keep his corner clean.

Unfortunately, that didn't leave a lot of time to work with Jase and Emma. Jase had gotten a little apartment in Cedar Key, but he had to go back to Gainesville on weekdays to teach again. Emma was working and living out at Seahorse Key most of the week. They met on weekends and continued to plan the Rosewood reunion and cemetery dedication. Roy, however, was starting to question why he was even doing it, exhausted and sore as he was every time he went to meet them after a week of hard labor, working double time to harvest clams in case red tide seeped his way. He liked Emma—really liked her—but there was never a reprise of the kiss from that first evening. He'd popped a mint and leaned in more than a few times since that one moon-intoxicated night, but so far she'd given every indication that it was to be a one-time event.

And no wonder. He was a fisherman. A war hero, sure, and the army taught him that he was a worthy man, an exceptional leader, a caregiver, a skilled tactical officer, and a supportive team player. But the lifelong effects of those days in the military weren't easy for other folks to understand. Most people he met couldn't see beyond "fighting a war" to understand the rest of it: That any doubts his pa ever planted in him about African Americans, Asians, Jews, Latinos, or any other race of people were washed right out the window when he trained and fought with his brothers of every color, day in and day out, forming a bond the cut right through the superficial boundaries of race. And they definitely didn't get that being out there in the Middle East to fight those "Ay-rabs," as his pa used to call them, also opened his eyes to a whole new culture of kind, decent, and terrified people who had families and vocations and dreams just like anyone else. And like the rest of us, they were at the mercy of forces beyond their control. No one could comprehend what it felt like to be unable to protect the "incidentals," the civilians who were in the wrong place at the wrong time. They weren't all a bunch of jihadists, he quickly discovered. They were mothers and fathers and, oh, so many innocent children. He couldn't bear to hear the mothers crying when their children were pierced by shrapnel. The lucky ones died immediately, but many—too many—died screaming, tortured deaths in their helpless mother's arms, or were left with a lifetime of agonizing pain, disability, and trauma. Sometimes it reminded him of the guttural sobs he often heard his mother try to stifle late at night. He understood the despair as close as his own. Could Emma understand that? Could Jase?

Anyway, after the war, his "war hero" status didn't add up to much beyond a medal, a modest disability check, free health care at the VA with the added touch of long hours spent in waiting rooms, and an occasional "thank you for your service" from a stranger. Those "thank you's" felt hollow to Roy, even when offered sincerely. No one, not even a military person or a grateful civilian, could fully comprehend what it felt like to be the only one left. *Especially when I did everything, everything, in my power to protect my brothers. My best friends.* No one could imagine his sense of loss and his loneliness.

He liked Emma, but he knew she only saw a clumsy, uneducated fisherman and a wounded warrior. His deformity surely repulsed her. No wonder there hadn't been another kiss. He would never be good enough for her.

And he liked Jase too—once his best buddy and certainly his only surviving one—but Jase was a professor now. He was as unlike a soldier or a commercial fisherman as a person could be, not to mention his close ties to Rosewood and his relatives buried in the cemetery. Then it turned out it was Emma's bloodline too. It made sense for those two to work on this project. Besides, Emma and Jase knew how to work with the archeologist, the Historical Society, the city commission, and all of the other professional folks. Roy, by comparison, didn't even have a decent pair of non-clamming boots to meet people in.

Roy allowed himself to wallow deeper into the consideration of his insufficiencies. He was the only son of a Ku Klux Klan grand wizard. The legless, ashamed descendant of two myopically proud, self-righteous bigots. These days, postwar, he just knew fishing. And surviving. And taking care of Ma. He had nothing to offer. In fact, based on his history and his family curse, he decided right then and there that the best way he could help right the wrongs of everything was to do nothing at all. Stay out of it. The cemetery would be in better hands without him, Emma was better off working just with Jase than worrying about how much Roy liked her, and with red tide literally around the corner, he had to focus on just surviving. Not letting everything die. *Again.*

And then, as he fired the winch and started rhythmically pulling up his clam bags, he saw something troubling enough to pull him out of his downward spiral. *Molgula* sea squirts—hundreds of them—were weighing down the outside of his nets, pulling the buoys down and making the bags hard to haul. This was nothing new: clam bags filled to the brim with thriving clams seemed to be the ideal substrate for tunicates, and he was used to plucking them off, haul after haul, as they squirted him unrelentingly from their taut little translucent brown siphons. Because of his knowledge about sea squirts that Jase had imbued him with so many years ago, he was much gentler with them than most clammers were, peeling them off and trying not to crush them under his boots. But these tunicates were not well. They looked desiccated, gray, flaccid, and were barely squirting.

He dropped his net bags and pointed his bird dog to Seahorse Key. He forgot about feeling like a fuck-up. Like him, he knew that Emma was working overtime at the lab in response to whatever the hell was going on in the water lately, and she needed to know about this right away.

Seagrasses
....

Healthy seagrasses are a crucial part of the Gulf ecosystem. These submerged carpets of flowering plants help stabilize the seafloor, provide habitat and food to a wide variety of marine organisms, and contribute to keeping the water clean and well-oxygenated.

Of about seven regularly identified species in the eastern and southern Gulf, the two most abundant types of seagrass are turtle grass (*Thalassia testudinum*) and manatee grass (*Syringodium filiforme*), named after the animals that love them the most. Turtle grass is flat and ribbon-like and is a favorite food of the green sea turtle. Manatee grass, by comparison, is thin and cylindrical-shaped, and is a perfect and tasty nutrient source for the West Indian manatee. Both can be easily spotted in healthy shallow waters as large "lawns" of underwater greenspace, and both teem with life.

On days with better water visibility, it is worthwhile to don a mask and snorkel and gently float over a shallow seagrass bed. A wonderland of life will be revealed between, upon, and above the millions of blades of grass.

Chapter 20

CONNECTION (2022)

THE FALL SEMESTER was underway at the University of Florida, and Jase was back in Gainesville teaching for most of each week. The sounds of splashing cormorants, squawking seagulls and whining spin reels were replaced by the bells of Century Tower and the scuttle of thousands of busy students bustling through the stately, red-bricked campus. Jase was, at the moment, on a brisk walk between classes in an attempt to clear his head.

He'd been having a difficult time concentrating since his face-to-face with his great-grandfather, Sam Carter. He was an academic, a professor, and a historian, with the curious mind of a scientist and a heart devoted to justice and equity. Both his curiosity and his devotion were piqued to new levels with his first-ever experience with, well, what would you call it? He wasn't even sure. Interdimensional connection? He'd spent a few fruitless minutes Googling it, but just kept coming up with thousands of entries about either "possession" or "mediums." He was definitely not a medium, and while he had been temporarily immobilized, he'd hardly felt possessed during their heartfelt exchange.

Jase finally abandoned the need to define what happened and surrendered to the realization that, whatever it was, it was real. His lifetime of work, rooted in the tragic history of his family line, his traumatic childhood reality check, and his deep faith, had prepared him well. When he was thirteen and suddenly estranged from Roy and the island, his pastor had reassured him: "God works in mysterious ways." When he studied Zen Buddhism in college, he was struck by the tenet of "not knowing is most intimate." In other words, don't mar the power and mystery of his experience with research and labels. Sam had made it very clear: *Time is short. Don't think. Help.*

In the lecture hall, he was a well-loved instructor, known to hold wide-eyed undergraduates rapt with his powerful stories of Selma and Gandhi and Martin Luther King Junior's dream. He orated, in painful detail, the atrocities of the massacres, community dissolutions, and lynchings in Rosewood, Newberry, Perry, and right there in Gainesville, where a well-organized Ku Klux Klan group operated during the Reconstruction era and still today meets secretly in covert locations in the rural communities fifteen miles in any direction from the free-thinking island of the university.

Despite Jase's flair and fervor, history for most students still just came across as stories from a long time ago, not even remotely related to their current lives filled with classes and smart phones and friends and Netflix and exams and GPA's and dreams of their imminent careers. But this week, Jase had moved them. Something in his impassioned and almost spiritual delivery elicited in his students a state of earnestness. Young minds fortunate enough to receive his teachings bubbled and spilled over with evolved thoughts and fresh awareness:

No one should ever be treated that way, ever again. We are all too interconnected to allow it. Each of us is descended from an oppressed, or an oppressor, or even both. It's still going on. Maybe not via public lynchings anymore, but isn't it a fact that when I was in the grocery store yesterday, I saw a manager sternly ask a

*Latinx pre-med student to remove their hoodie while me and four
other white kids with hoodies just walked right by? Didn't that
young Muslim student in a hijab have her hand up in economics
class for like ten minutes this morning before giving up, while
the white male professor kept calling on other kids? Wasn't that
trans kid in the dining hall called a pussy by a frat brother? Did
I do anything about it? No. Did I accept a "Stop Asian Hate" sign
that people were freely giving out and join the rally at the Reitz
Union, where a Chinese American student had been wrongly
assaulted the day before for being a virus-carrier? No, I wanted
to go home, eat, watch some Tik Toks and study. I've been blind.
Wake up. Wake up!*

Waking up was happening all around Jase's orbit. He
walked over to the new historical marker erected in down-
town Gainesville, just steps away from where the Confederate statue of "Old Joe" had been torn down just a few years
ago. It was an essential marker in a prominent location, full
of important information about the history of lynchings in
Gainesville, and a memorial to eight of the thirteen or more
who had died in the area during Jim Crow. Unlike in his
great-grandpa's living time period, it was finally reasonably
safe to openly talk about this recent history, finally the time to
bridge the gap between his great-grandpa's dark days and the
days yet to come. He was glad he could reach young minds. He
thought of the community that showed up when the marker
was installed: youth leaders, pastors, rabbis, the mayor and
commissioners, and hundreds of diverse community members. Yes, it was time.

He also remembered, with a shudder, how when "Old Joe"
was brought down, a big enough faction of the community
made a real stink about it. In addition to the cheering residents
who happily bid old bigoted Joe goodbye, there was a smaller,

irate group that still managed to be plenty loud.

"You're removing history!" someone hollered.

"The South will rise again!" pronounced another.

He ignored them, considering them to be the last stubborn, furious bygones of a dying era. But then, like a dagger, Jase remembered a low, gruff voice that stabbed him right through his equanimity: "Fuck you, N—." When he turned his head to discover who'd fouled the air with that hateful epithet, he saw that the man was talking directly to *him*. Jase's eyes met two shockingly angry blue eyes, and held them while an unspoken conversation took place between the two men.

Jase: *No need for that kind of language. "Old Joe" isn't appropriate here. It's not history worth erecting a statue for. It's a dishonor.*

Blue Eyes: *It's MY history. My identity. You got no rights to take it.*

Jase: *What about MY rights? My history? Everything you took from ME?*

Blue Eyes: *Don't like it? Then go back to where you came from.*

Jase: *This is where I come from now, just like you after your European ancestors immigrated here. No difference.*

Blue Eyes: *Plenty of difference. This land is my land, not yours.*

Jase: *You really want this as your identity, man? Bigotry? Violence towards others based on their skin color? Debate about whose land this is? C'mon brother. Look around you. Time to move forward.*

Jase remembered detecting just a second or two of softening and shifting in the man's glinting blue eyes, a moment when all that focused hatred seemed to be diffused and replaced by something else—something that briefly broke the barrier between them.

But it was just a flash. A man next to him wearing a red ball cap and waving a confederate flag saw their eyes locked with one another and yelled, "What you lookin' at, Nig? C'mon, Clemson. Don't waste your time." The blue-eyed man's expression hardened, and the barricade was re-erected.

Jase walked away.

Marsh Periwinkles

The Cedar Keys are a major transition zone. Not only do the brackish waters feature the merging of salt- and freshwater habitats to form an estuary, but unlike the more famous, tropical Florida Keys, they lie at a unique latitude between subtropical and tropical ecosystems. For that reason, visitors can observe otherwise-disparate species living together.

This subtropical/tropical transition is especially evident at the waterline, where you might see more-northern marsh grasses (*Spartina alterniflora*), any of three possible tropical mangrove species, or a combination of the two.

Despite their proximity to one another in this unique ecosystem, both habitats retain their unique biomes. The salt marsh is the specific habitat for the marsh periwinkle (*Littorina irrorata*), also referred to as the marsh snail. The animal has a pleasing, classic snail shape, and Cedar Key periwinkles are sometimes sold through shell distributors for this reason. They are only found on marsh grasses, where they comb the blades for algae as they glide up and down with the tides.

Scientists discovered that the eyes of these snails are adapted for vertical vision, perfectly suited to life on a blade of grass. They will retract tightly into their shells when the tide is low, sometimes waiting in the sun for hours for high tide to return. However, as the water warms with climate change, these snails have been discovered climbing farther up the marsh grass to avoid the less-oxygenated warm water and escape new predators lured by the higher temperatures.

It is important for marsh snails to have some predators, as they would otherwise overgraze and decimate the marsh grasses, which provide important shoreline stabilization and water filtration. However, too many predators would also have a deleterious effect. The balance of the transitional ecosystem must be maintained. Marsh snails are beneficial to humans as well, as they are yet another important indicator species of environmental toxins.

Florida's Living Shoreline program is working to counteract the effects of climate change by restoring natural shorelines that have been wiped out due to sea-level rise and habitat degradation. The salt marsh ecosystem featuring the careful balance of *Spartina* and *Littorina* is a major focus of their efforts.

Perhaps the Cedar Keys can serve as a global model for what transition can be like, where seemingly different existences can evolve to thrive together in shared and harmonious bounty.

Chapter 21

RECKONING (2022)

EMMA HAD BEEN busy at the lab lately. Thunder buffeted the sky with unusual regularity most afternoons, and the wind made the marsh snails retreat to the base of the shoreline grasses, a sure indication that more rain was coming. Frequent storms rolled through in early December, well past the normal summer thunderstorm patterns and way past hurricane season, and the water was becoming much less salty as a result. The no-name storm that had caught Roy the day he met Emma had knocked out power for three days and beat up part of the research dock to the point that it had started to float away.

The storms were not only anomalous; they had become ominous, wreaking havoc on the normal salinity patterns of regular flushing from the Gulf that far offshore from the main estuary. The Suwannee River was pouring out way more freshwater than usual, keeping salinity from rising to optimal levels, and Emma's echinoderms were unhappy. Still, extended hyposaline stress alone couldn't explain the increasing frequency of diseases, and now mortality, that Emma was finding almost daily in a wider array of organisms. As a result, she was shifting her focus to marine biochemistry. She believed that there had to be either chemicals or microorganisms at work, which, combined with the low salinity, was too much for a whole gamut of marine life to adapt to.

It reminded her of what had happened in the Indian River

Lagoon on Florida's east coast just a few years prior. Manatees had just been taken off the endangered species list, even though the unholy trinity of pollution, habitat destruction, and climate change was intensifying. At the same time that the feds proclaimed manatee population levels to be adequate, Emma and other biologists were detecting troubling changes in the health of the invertebrates in the lagoon, along with changes in water temperature, salinity, and chemistry. They begged policymakers to reconsider the status of the manatees and put stricter regulations on polluters and developers, but their protestations were met with dismissive nods, a salute to the higher manatee population numbers, and new items on the agenda. Today, Emma realized somberly, the manatees are dying off at an alarming rate, trying unsuccessfully to survive by eating the less-nutritious, less calorie-dense algae that clogged the Indian River Lagoon. She was starting to see the same algae in increasing amounts right here, as the marine and aquatic grasses withered away. All the signs were here now, in the Cedar Keys. If she could take the Indian River timeline and present it to policymakers with real data from these waters, there might be a chance for salvation, or at least some kind of basic regulation, this time.

She was loading her skiff with small jars to sample water at various checkpoints around the island when she heard a piercing whistle. It definitely wasn't the familiar sweet whistle of the osprey couple perched high in their stick-nest atop a pole by the research dock. She froze, knowing the offending sound of that kind of whistle too well, then turned. There, on the boat dock, was a burly and unkempt man, with steel-blue eyes fixed on her like a predator. *Shit.* Where was Andrew the ranger? Kenny the lighthouse keeper? The university students? Today was Sunday, usually a day off for them. She was alone. Her work had become more intense with the quickly deteriorating health of the marine life around the island, so she had come out on a Sunday knowing she might be the only one on the island. Now, she regretted that choice.

Emma disguised her nerves under an official-sounding response: "Sir, Seahorse Key is a wildlife refuge and is off limits to private boaters except on open house days in October and July. If you're interested in coming here then, you can find all of the information on the website." She gestured towards a covered area with picnic tables and touch tanks. "Feel free to take a brochure from the information table under the pavilion before you leave."

The man said, "tsk, tsk," and spit into the grass as he lifted and lowered a gravel-filled bucket nearby, for the sole purpose of displaying his well-pumped muscles. "You can call me Clem, doll. 'Sir' is way too formal a way to be between us." Emma shuddered, reflecting almost wistfully on that day when Roy similarly tried to show his muscles. He had been so oafy and comical by contrast. This guy was sinister. "Hmm," he continued in a slow local drawl. "Looks like you might be needin' someone to help you start that outboard. Don't worry, beautiful. I'm here."

Where in the hell did he get the idea that I needed help? thought Emma, watching nervously as he walked towards her. Reflexively, she put her hand up. "No thanks, sir, um, Clem. I got it. Now please exit the island before I call the ranger. You can be fined for being here during non-public days." The ranger wasn't there, she knew, but hopefully he didn't.

"I like it when you say my name, beautiful. And I don't see no ranger nowhere. Looks like it's just you an' me. And ain't you a pretty one! Where you from, anyway, love? Mexico? China?"

Emma hardened. "I'm Native American," she replied coldly. "From right on this ground where we stand."

Clem seemed to think this was hilarious. "Ha ha! Oh, a feisty Injun, are we? Why not let me come over there and show you how to start an engine, Injun, if you know what I mean...." A bulge in his pants was growing bigger. Emma felt sick as he advanced, and even though he was much larger than she was, she was more than ready to hurt him if she had to.

Roy, meanwhile, had just made the turn to approach Seahorse Key. An unusually large number of dolphins jumped in his wake, making worried clicking noises he hadn't heard before. They seemed nervous and uneasy. He caught sight of a large, white boat at the dock. It was a fancy, drafty boat for these shallow waters, and it was unusual to see a private passenger vessel moored there on a non-open house day. Disquieted, he pulled out his binoculars and had a look. It was a Grady White. *A Grady White!* A large Grady White like that around here could only belong to one person. Roy had been going at half-speed, mindful of manatees and the shoals shifting with the changing tide. But now he opened the throttle, wishing he'd serviced his boat engine last week like he was supposed to. It sputtered in protest, but managed to accelerate while Roy continued to scan the dock area through his binoculars.

There. He spotted them by Emma's skiff. A bulky Clem Dawes was barreling towards Emma, whose hand was thrust outward in defense. Roy was incensed and a bit panicked; even from this far out, he could see that Emma was in trouble. He started yelling furiously and squawking his emergency airhorn. Clem, distracted by the annoying racket, turned his head angrily towards the approaching bird dog. Taking advantage of the distraction, Emma shoved him over the edge of the dock, his mass parting the school of silver-backed baitfish in two. She quickly jumped aboard her skiff, started the engine, and hightailed it towards Roy.

Roy was overjoyed. He threw her a line and brought her skiff into his gunwale as she cut the engine and jumped aboard and into his arms. "Yes!" he cheered, planting a deep kiss on her unprotesting lips. "Good move, there, lady!" She kissed him back, suddenly feeling giddy. Still holding each other close, they watched and laughed as a red-faced, enraged Clem Dawes swam over to his big Grady White and flopped on board. As he started his engine and sped their way, Roy was feeling thick with bravado. He pulled Emma close again, kissed her, and held up his middle finger to starboard, in Clem's plain view.

Clem shouted menacingly at them while he roared by at a speed way too fast for bucolic, manatee-filled waters. "You're fucking DEAD, Roy Bamford the fucking THIRD! What would your pa and grandpa do, seein' you suckin' face with' an Injun? He'd fucking KILL you, that's what, and so will I!"

They might have let his threats get to them, but they didn't have time. Clem slammed into a sand shoal with his big, drafty boat and was firmly grounded. "SHIT TO HELL!!!!!" he roared, stomping around the deck, throwing beer bottles and life jackets around in frustration. Roy and Emma couldn't stop laughing.

"I'll call you a Sea Tow," shouted Roy with an insincere smile as he maneuvered back towards the lab. "But seeing as the tide is goin' out, it may be another six to eight hours or so...." Clem glared at him murderously, but Roy was emboldened by his newfound swagger. It felt exciting to beat the alpha for a change. In truth, he felt like it was actually him and Emma who were the alphas, together, untouchable against the evils of the world, and that truly aroused him.

When they got back to the dock, they were still laughing, high on relief and victory. Roy forgot about the sick tunicates. He forgot that Clem Dawes had just threatened to murder him, had clearly said his full name and knew who his pa was. He was just so happy that Emma was all right that he wanted her as close as she could get to him, right there and then. Emma too forgot about the worsening Gulf, her critical water sampling, her indignation. Together they had triumphed against a racist, misogynistic bully, and to her, that was a win she'd longed for most of her life, and one that could help change the world. The reality of having a genuine ally in Roy excited her.

When Roy interlaced his hand with hers, she reciprocated. They entered the old lab and tumbled, giggling, into a worn, half-puffed-up inflatable dinghy in the back corner of the room, underneath a floor-to-wall bookshelf. A dislodged, dusty, fourth edition of *Taxonomy of Gulf Copepods* fell right on top of them. Roy flung the book, the raft's oars, and his prosthetic leg overboard with a clatter, making them both laugh all the more. He turned to face her, suddenly struck quiet by the tenderness and desire in her eyes. He almost looked over his shoulder. *Is she really looking at me like that?* He allowed his eyes to connect with hers and linger there for a few seconds.

"Hello, spirit woman," he whispered. Emma could smell the hint of potato chips and mints on his breath as he confessed, "I'm, um, a little out of practice." Emma simply sighed, extended her fingers to his hairline, and stroked his disheveled gray-blonde curls behind his ears. He tasted her lips. Salty, like the Gulf they were surrounded by on all sides. Pliant, like the movement of seagrasses in the currents. He ventured further, and as the heat of his breath found the side of her neck, she melted completely in his arms. Their lovemaking was natural and easy, filled with a sense of rightness and authenticity that neither of them had ever experienced before. It aligned with the intimate cadence of the tides' ebb and flow, the vibration of every atom, the pulsating beat of nature. Just one primordial rhythm.

A half-hour later, Emma and Roy lay together in the womb of the small vinyl boat as their breathing steadied. Emma had her two legs wrapped around Roy's single one, and was delicately tracing the nub of his other leg with her fingers, which felt surprisingly wonderful to him. Roy had never done a good job containing himself with Emma, and so in keeping with that, he blurted out, "I love you, Emateloya Tiger."

She laughed at his mispronunciation, touched that he would even honor her by trying, and surprised herself by returning the sentiment. "Wow, Roy Bamford the Third. It looks like I love you too."

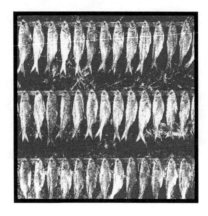

Baitfish
....

Few animals get as little attention as the lowly baitfish. While fishermen pine for the biggest grouper, the fattest shark, and the longest snook, thousands of baitfish school in silvery masses beneath them, providing the essential link in the food web needed to cultivate any prize fish.

In Florida's Gulf, the main species of baitfish are glass minnow anchovies (*Anchoa mitchilli*) and the American shad (*Alosa sapidissima*), also known as menhaden. One of the most exciting things to witness in a healthy Gulf habitat is feeding time, usually right around dusk. As the sun begins to settle and colors paint the western sky, keep an eye out for breaks in the calm surface that look like patches of boiling water as the small fish frantically try to escape feasting predators. If not for their healthy, fertile populations, the food web would be irreparably broken, and the top-shelf fish would quickly starve into nonexistence.

Safety tip: while it can be very enjoyable to snorkel through schools of baitfish in shallow waters during midday, it is not advisable to do so at dusk when the baitfish are sure to be the main course.

Chapter 22

PREPARATIONS (2022)

IN THE WEEKS that followed Roy and Emma spent their days scrambling madly to harvest clams and collect samples while red tide seeped and curled ever closer to them in the warming waters. They spent their nights making love, while Jase squeezed midterm-exam proctoring in with intensive preparation for the New Year's Day Rosewood centennial. The three spent Christmas with Roy's Ma, exchanging gifts, cooking, and feasting, catching each other up while working to finalize the many details involved with bringing several hundred Rosewood descendants and their families to the tiny fishing village.

Jase had barely seen Roy and Emma in the month leading up to the holidays, and was pleased to note the very obvious development in their relationship. The long, endearing looks, the entwined fingers, and the close body contact were impossible to ignore. Ma was clearly overjoyed, and crying a whole lot. "Oh, just look at you two! Like young sweethearts, you are!" she'd exclaim. "Roy, you've waited so long for true love. Better late than never, as they say. It just makes my heart so happy!"

Roy was a bit embarrassed, but couldn't argue with the truth of what she was saying, so he simply responded, "Ma, Ma, no need to cry..."

Jase was happy for them too, and also grateful for his own busy-ness. It made him forget his loneliness. He had been very productive these past weeks, and was excited to fill them in on his progress.

"Every apartment surrounding the city beach park is booked for the reunion," he reported. "Some of the elders felt some trepidation about coming to a place they consider to be a sundown town, but after a whole lot of coaxing, and with the blessing of Ms. Altamese Wrispus, the reunion chairwoman, we got them all on board. We reserved the park and notified the local police of our intention to hold a major event there. The reunion committee hired a blues band for New Year's Eve and a gospel choir for New Year's Day, which falls on a Sunday. We're starting to put flyers up around town so folks know what to expect and feel welcome to attend too."

"You sure that's a good idea?" An image of Clem Dawes emerged from the scary backwoods of Roy's mind. He hadn't seen the guy in weeks, and could only hope that Clem was so embarrassed by their last encounter that he had retreated back to Bronson to lick his wounds for a while. That thought offered little consolation, though. Roy recalled Jase's somber recounting of the history of Rosewood, when Klan members who harbored years of conditioned hatred needed only a single lie to justify their ruthless destruction of good people.

"Yes, yes. It'll be fine," Jase assured him. "The Rosewood Family Reunion has always been open to all, and this year, because it's the centennial, it's getting actual publicity for a welcome change. We're practically taking over the public city park for two days. Let's make it a celebration—a festival even—let everyone know we don't want to hide anymore, and we don't want to continue all of this separation. We want to move forward, towards a future of truth and healing, and everyone's invited to celebrate with us."

Emma approved. It was the way of her tribe too: heal the wounds, learn from the past, stand up proudly, and evolve.

Roy, however, was still baffled. *Why aren't the Rosewood descendants furious? Why would they make themselves vulnerable again? They should be up in arms, demanding their land be given back, demanding respectful treatment—not having a barbecue.* But the decision was not his to make. All he could do was be watchful.

Roy, Emma, and Ma listened attentively as Jase continued recounting an impressive list of completed tasks. He'd called the press to cover the centennial in an effort to raise awareness beyond the walls of his classroom. He'd even invited his students to come. He'd raided the city records and worked with Dr. Gonzalez-Tennant to locate and identify the unmarked graves of almost one hundred former African American residents of Cedar Key, including all of his great-grandpa's cousins. The memorial signs were already made and would be installed on December 30. And the Rosewood landowner had given permission for them to come onto the grounds and the cemetery for the ceremony there. Everything was ready.

"What about Sam?" asked Emma. It had been months since their initial encounter at Cemetery Point Park.

"I've been to Adeline's stone a few times these past weeks," Jase replied, "Keeping him up to date. I've been feeling like I was just talking to the air though..."

Emma reassured him. "I haven't felt anything as heavy as we did in the summertime. Have you, Ma?"

"It's been sad but steady," she concurred. "Sam must be hearing you, Jase."

Jase brightened. "Well, see, that's the thing! One day just last week I started *hearing* him. Like really hearing him, his voice, even though I couldn't see him! He told me he'd been talkin' to me all along, and suddenly I just started hearing him. He said he didn't get it either, that no one else seemed to ever hear him. But hey—God works in mysterious ways, you know?"

While the others were surprised, Emma was jubilant. "Jase, that's wonderful! It's kind of like when the dolphins talked to me that day, and asked me to connect with Sam. Not our place to figure it out. We just allow it; we trust."

"Emma, if not for that moment of connection between the two of you, Sam might still be in some kind of purgatory, stuck in the bottom of the boat channel," Jase replied gratefully. "We may be evidence-based academics, but I think we can both accept that we don't need to know exactly how some things happen. I'm just glad they do."

"You've done so much, man! Sorry we ain't been more help," offered Roy. "We've been a little busy."

A mischievous glimmer sparkled in Jase's eyes as he smiled at Roy and Emma sitting hip-to-hip. "Yea, brother, I can see you and my cousin been a little busy...."

Roy reddened. "Nah, nah, man, that's not what I'm talking about, although...." he squeezed Emma's hand and looked over at her bashfully as she tilted her head towards him with a lovely smile. "Seriously. It's been rough for clamming lately."

"Been a scramble at the lab, too," added Emma. "Feels like I'm racing time with the water changing so quickly, the algae increasing, and the marine animals showing more diseases and failure to thrive. Just yesterday, I saw a cormorant actually spit a fish out. I cast netted the fish while it was still stunned, and found its stomach contents full of plastic. I'm trying to get my data to the Fish and Wildlife Commission by the end of the year. There's just no more time to lose."

Roy nodded. "I've harvested and sold about every last clam bag I've got, just racin' the red tide. My hands hurt, my back hurts, but it's done, and now I can help you out a lot more." His eyes shifted. "I only pray for a better new year..."

Jase seemed to sense Roy's uneasiness. "What is it, buddy? Seems like there's something you're not telling me."

Roy confessed, "I'm worried about some less-than-savory characters inviting themselves to the party, that's all. You know that guy Clemson Dawes who harassed us in Rosewood, the same one who threatened me and Emma a couple of weeks ago? He's been suspiciously quiet since. I did a few surveillance drives over by the Scratch Bar and Clem's red truck has been there a lot, and there've been a few more cars there than usual lately."

Jase looked uneasy. "The Scratch Bar? What's that?"

Roy chuckled contemptuously. "Been there since my grandaddy's days. Just a literally stinkin' hole in the wall, tucked back between some oyster houses. My pa used to take me there, told me I could be part of the 'club.' I found out his daddy had started that club—the Cedar Key KKK—and he was the self-proclaimed grand wizard. Didn't take me long to put two and two together and stay the hell away from there. Can't believe it's even still open after all these years, that the health department hasn't shut it down."

Both Emma and Jase's eyes widened with surprise and concern. Ma sat in stern silence. Roy continued, "This is the first time I've said it out loud, all this time. Ain't somethin' I'm proud of."

"I think there are a lot of things you haven't told us, Roy," Emma said gently. "And now I'm starting to understand a little more about why I like you."

Roy was surprised, having expected at least some level of shock and disdain after revealing his shameful truth. "Huh?"

"You're *brave*, Roy," she continued. "That's a hard thing to talk about."

"I'll say," said Jase. "Honestly, man, if I'd known that back when we were kids, well...."

Roy bristled. If Jase had known that, maybe they could have protected Jase's family. Maybe his dad would have been all right. Maybe they would have had more summers. Then again, maybe Jase would've never been his friend at all. "I couldn't stand to tell you, man," he admitted. "It was easier for me to just forget it. In fact, I barely even understood it myself, until, well...your dad." There was a heavy pause.

Ma started crying. "I'm so proud of you son. You made a choice after that. You walked away. Your daddy was furious as the hounds of hell, but you walked away."

Roy touched Ma's shoulder and gave her a tender, sad look. He said, "I don't know if the bar is still considered some sort of pathetic headquarters, after all these years, or if Clem even knows its infamous history, being from Bronson and all. But I do know that some pretty gnarly guys hang out there, sometimes all day, mostly gettin' drunk, talkin' trash, and I know Clem's there all the time."

"He knows," said Ma somberly. "The Dawes family used to live in Cedar Key. I remember his daddy. Horrible man."

Jase added, "Strange that he lives in Bronson now. That's actually a really great town for race relations, you know. It was one of the first to be integrated in this part of the state, and never had the kinds of major issues between blacks, whites, and Latinos that other Florida small towns have dealt with. Doesn't seem like a match for Clemson."

"Maybe that's why he's spending all of his time here lately, who knows?" Roy said. "The man is clearly wealthy. Maybe he's got land out there or something Cedar Key ain't got. Shit, maybe he's thinkin' about moving back here? Either way, I'd feel better if he were far, far away."

Jase said, "Glad you said something. Other than getting a permit from the police department, I hadn't thought about formal security for the Rosewood centennial until now. Maybe we should think about assigning some folks to be inconspicuous bouncers at the city park, you know, to keep an eye out for suspicious people or activity."

Emma, rubbing Roy's back reassuringly, concurred. "That's a good idea, Jase. Maybe we should think about a few plain clothes security folks, you know, a few people who are aware and alert. I'll volunteer. We've only got a few days before a whole lot of people show up here."

Meanwhile, just a few miles away at the Scratch Bar, the man in question, Clemson Dawes, the new de facto Grand Wizard of the freshly revived unofficial Levy County Cedar Key chapter of the Ku Klux Klan, was leading a meeting of about eight highly inebriated members.

"Y'all seen the flyers?" he hissed. "We got a whole lot of unwelcome folks comin' to town next weekend. They think they can just waltz in here, take things over like it's *their* town? Guess they still ain't learned nothin'. They is SO gonna be sorry. This is our big chance. Look at ol' Sam Carter's watch, boys. It's time to rally!"

The murmured response of the group was less enthusiastic than Clem would have liked. He tried again: "Are you boys ready to rally or what? Kick some black ass?" The drunks looked uneasy. Clem's temples began to pulse. "I thought we was gonna do something about this! Reestablish the honorable mission of the Levy County Cedar Key chapter, remember? What in the hell is wrong with you guys?"

Roy the Second's old friend at the end of the bar finally spoke up. He chose his words carefully, in part because he didn't want to offend a volatile Clem and in part because he was totally schnockered. "Clem, it's a different time now, man. It ain't like before, when this part of the world was a no-man's land. Shit, even back in the eighties when Roy the Second roughed up that black university man, he caught all sorts of flack and got prison time. It ain't the same anymore, Clem. If we just go and rough up a bunch of black people here when there're news cameras and witnesses all around and everything, the only thing we're gonna accomplish is going to prison, and making us look bad. I got only a few good years left, man, and I sure as hell don't wanna spend them behind bars. Do you?"

Clem was indignant. He addressed the remaining chapter members through clenched teeth. "What the hell?! Do you men hear this bullshit?" They looked down at their bottles. "I don't get it!" he hollered, red-faced and exasperated. "What about everything we've been talkin' about all these months since I started comin' here? And you, old-timer, my grandaddy Clark Dawes lived here, fished here, taught me everything I know, and you're tryin' to tell me how things are these days?!" Clem was indignant. "We've got a golden opportunity here at our stinkin' doorstep, and y'all just wanna sit here and keep drinking' and talkin'? No action?"

The elder drunk spoke with a seasoned, slightly slurred clarity. "Clem, we was just talkin'. Winos in a rotting bar is what this so-called 'chapter' is all about these days, man— livin' out our Aryan fantasies with what few of us are left. Your granddaddy Dawes—I remember him. I was young, but hell, he was hard to forget. But man, listen now, the world is changing. This is about the only safe place left to talk the way we talk without gettin' arrested. Acting on it would be suicide. Just accept it man. Let the coloreds have their event. They ain't hurtin' no one. They ain't movin' in. They'll be gone all on their own by Monday, and we can all sit here and get plastered and bitch about it."

Clem, speechless, was turning scarlet. Finally, he spat on the floor and screamed, "Fuck you ALL! You pansy betrayers. FUCK. YOU. ALL!"

The old man stood up unsteadily and faced Clem, looking him right in the eye. "Clem, you're still a fairly young man. You got money, you got health, you got a lotta life ahead of you. Take my advice. Let this go."

Clemson Dawes took a step forward. He punched the old man hard in the nose and stormed out, leaving the elder bleeding out on the floor.

Double-Crested Cormorant
· ·

It is common to hear newcomers to inshore Gulf waters gasp with surprise when a cormorant, floating peacefully on the surface, suddenly disappears below the water, sometimes not reemerging for over one minute. Just as the observer begins to lose hope, the bird pops up a few feet away, usually maneuvering a sizable fish down its gullet.

Double-crested cormorants (*Phalacrocorax auritus)* are regular residents of Cedar Key. They can most commonly be observed fishing from the as described, standing atop pilings drying their outstretched wings in the breeze, or roosting in trees.

Cormorant populations have rebounded after significant declines in the 19th century due to hunting and then again in the 20th century from DDT poisoning. While populations in the Gulf of Mexico have become stable, they are once again under threat, this time from entanglement by fishing lines and increased plastics in the ocean. The birds ingest these plastics over time, leading to sickness and painful death.

If we can reduce environmental stressors and pollutants, we will be giving ourselves the pleasure of enjoying these entertaining fisher birds for a long time to come.

Chapter 23

THE ROSEWOOD CENTENNIAL (2023)

MS. ALTAMESE WRISPUS—CHAIRWOMAN of the Rosewood Family Reunion Inc. and, at ninety-three years of age, the eldest of the Rosewood descendants—smoothed out the silver sequins of her dress a few moments before the opening prayer on the thirty-six thousand, five hundredth morning since the Rosewood massacre. It was a fresh, achingly beautiful New Year's morning, and as the pastor proclaimed his thanks for the grace of this day and the blessing of being together, dolphins reverently rolled their shiny backs in the shallow waters off the city beach for all to see.

Folks had arrived in droves the day before from all parts east, north and south, settling into their rooms, heading out on island and bird-watching boat tours, and gathering at sunset for grouper sandwiches, barbecued chicken and corn at the city beach park on New Year's Eve. They spent the evening feasting and dancing and hugging one another. The blues band that Jase had hired from Gainesville played on a trailered bird dog fashioned into a stage, and their sizzling music brought even some of the elders to their feet. The park was so lit with festivity that locals and tourists drifted over, and soon visitors from Europe, New York, Wisconsin, and Japan were dancing and celebrating with lighthearted locals and Rosewood family members alike.

Roy, Emma, Jase, and a small group of security guards kept a sharp eye out for unruly characters; fortunately, everything ran smoothly almost to the countdown to midnight. Roy only had to escort one inebriated local senior named Jimmy Junior off to some garbage cans to barf, relieved that his worst offense was to start yelling at the band, "Fuck bein' white; I shoulda been born a brother! I love black-man blues music! This is fucking AWESOME! Happy Fucking New Year!!" Roy pulled Jimmy Junior away gingerly and tucked him in with a blanket from his truck on a bench near the stage, where he promptly passed out.

While Roy was tending to Jimmy Junior, Emma was looking around for Roy. The countdown was about to start, and she wanted to enjoy it with him. She spotted Jase and asked, "Jase, have you seen Roy?"

Jase gestured towards the garbage cans across the parking lot, in the direction of the city boat ramp. Emma saw Roy's silhouette, waved and called out to him, and headed his way. Roy waved back just as a big red truck pulled up between them.

The window was down, and Emma spotted Clem's muscled and eagle-tattooed forearm hanging out. She froze. Clem spat on the ground. "Where are you going, darlin'?" He grabbed her forcefully, pulling her small frame up to the truck and pinning her to the door. "We got some business, you and me and that N-loving boyfriend of yours. You two got some serious balls tryin' to mess with me, sweetheart."

"Emma?" Roy called out with concern, approaching the truck from the other side. "Um, you all right, my love?"

'Clem rolled down the other window. "Oh your 'love' is just fine, asshole," he answered. "In fact, she's the prettiest Injun I ever seen. Think I'm gonna take her home now and then when I'm done with her, I'm gonna come back and kill your traitor ass. And if either of you two got a problem with that, I ain't got a problem using *this*." He brandished a good-sized filet knife.

Roy saw Clem's other arm gripping Emma tightly against the side of the truck. He felt the familiar hot prickles on the back of his neck, and a confident power rose inside of him that he hadn't felt since his earlier days in the Gulf War. "Not today, Clem—!" he bellowed, racing across the parking lot. "Not today!"

But by the time he got around to the driver's side of the truck, Emma was already holding Clem's twisted arm at a painful angle against the door with one hand, while her other hand brandished the knife perilously close to the artery pulsing at his wrist. "Any questions?" she asked him disdainfully.

Both Roy and Clem were clearly caught off guard as Clem shouted, "What the fucking hell? OW! You bitch! Let me go!"

"I'll keep this, thank you," replied Emma as she pocketed the knife, punched him in the nose with the same hand, and let his twisted arm go. She kicked the truck hard as he floored the gas pedal. "You don't belong here!" she shouted after him, smoothed out her hair, and turned to face Roy.

"Um, Roy? Sweetheart? Are you okay?"

Roy shook his head, rendered momentarily speechless by the intense combination of relief and disappointment rushing through him. "I was gonna beat him up. I was gonna save you," he said, almost chuckling. "Guess not. Where'd you learn how to do that?"

Emma laughed. "Oh Roy," she bubbled, "There's a lot we still don't know about each other. Stick around so we can find out?"

Roy relaxed, feeling his amped-up testosterone and adrenaline slowly replaced by all the love chemicals. "Yes, yes, for sure!"

Emma grabbed his hand with a strong grip. How had he never noticed how strong she was before? "I love you," he said.

She smiled. "I love you too. Let's bring in the new year." They ambled back to the festivities, their strong hands intertwined, and kissed for a long time as the year overturned.

After the countdown and cheers that followed, a beautiful and well-spoken mother of seven from Lacoochee named Ebony Pickett approached the microphone. She was one of the main spokespersons for the Rosewood families and the granddaughter of Ms. Altamese Wrispus. "One hundred years ago tonight, our recent ancestors enjoyed a New Year's Eve gathering just like this one. They feasted and danced and warmed each other's hearts on a very cold night. There were even some white neighbors, Mr. Wright and his family, who joined in..."

She paused and joined in the group's friendly laughter as the not-quite-passed-out-after-all Jimmy Junior suddenly raised his head and hollered, "Mr. Right! Ladies, that's MEEEEEE!"

She continued, "They tucked their sweet children into bed in their cozy homes for the very last time." The group, including Jimmy Junior, fell silent. "Sleep well, dearest family and friends, as we give thanks to the Lord for our warm beds and for one another. Tomorrow morning, we will meet here, we will remember, and we will honor our heritage. For one hundred years, we have remained standing. Now, it is time for us to MOVE. It is high time for us all to walk together towards a brighter future—for our Rosewood families, and for everyone."

With unspoken deference, the group drifted back to their hotel rooms, and one-by-one their windows overlooking the beach park went dark. Except for the loud snoring coming from the park bench, tender silence descended on the night. An expansive moon watched over all, delaying its setting until after a pastel dawn broke at seven o'clock and a gospel choir from Otter Creek stepped in front of the bird dog stage. They began singing morning hymns in angelic harmony, arousing everyone from slumber. By eight o'clock, the crowd from the night before had returned. After helping themselves to warming cups of coffee and cocoa from the food tent, they found chairs in rows set like pews in front of the stage, and sat in meditation until the morning prayer began.

Ms. Altamese Wrispus had a folded paper ready. When the New Year's prayer was completed with an "Amen," Emma and Jase helped her to her feet and she approached the podium. After taking a few moments to adjust her hat, open the paper, and affix her reading glasses, she recited a poem called "The Rosewood Story" that she'd written many years ago.

In Rosewood, January 1, 1923, stood a village deep in the Suwannee River swamps. Our own black community. There were churches, a school, a Black fraternal lodge hall, a sugar mill, turpentine still and a store. A population of 150 or more.

A shattering scream came like a dream. I'll just call her Fannie Magdalene. A white woman cried to her friends so loud, "I know he was black, and that's a fact." That one statement drew the crowd.

Can you imagine how she said, "That black man took my money and fled." Let me tell you instead, how my family said it happened.

Fannie's white lover is the one who fled, taking her money, and slapping her side the head. Blood boiled, anger brewed, when Fannie's story was told her way, many lives had to pay. A bloody massacre commenced they say. Beatings, hangings, burnings, running. Until the seventh day.

Sympathetic whites hid our families by night. "Give up," they said, "you can't win this fight." Soldiers guarded our families as the train pulled in, bearing the burden of Fannie's unforgotten sin.

Seven days left a vanished town. History buried all around. For sixty-four years Rosewood was kept a secret; no one talked, black nor white. Neither wanted to restart that fight.

But since July 1985, our families meet yearly, to show love and unity dearly. With God on our side, and a great sense of pride, we have met in Washington D.C., in July '93. Then we stood in '94, in the presence of Florida's great legislators and more.

Yes! We stand strong, proud and free. For we are the Rosewood family!

The crowd exploded in cheers so resounding that Sam could hear them all the way to the cemetery. It was too much; he desperately wanted to attend. His steady presence seemed to have had a calming effect over time on the still-skittish friends and relatives all around him. If he left, he was worried that they would revert again into madness, but the sounds of his living kin were very tempting, and he figured it would be fine to spend a little bit of time with them. When Jase and his crew had installed the memorial signs and grave markers the day before, the spirits seemed to become more serene, and a few even started to transform from chaotic energy into their human shapes again. They would be fine, he reasoned, for just a few hours.

Once he reached the city park, he marveled at the sense of calm celebration, warmth, and love between both friends and strangers. Sam then felt a new sensation, an energy that was something between alive and dead, and found himself hovering over the hung over, snoring man on the bench.

The man was an elder known locally as Jimmy Junior, the

son of Jimmy the Greek Kepote who had a popular ice cream parlor on the island back in the Jim Crow days. Jimmy the Greek Senior was an immigrant who flatly refused to segregate his black customers in a "coloreds section" of his ice cream parlor, and Jimmy Junior never knew, growing up, the kind of intolerance that was rampant in communities all around Cedar Key. Despite an idyllic childhood, he had a hard life after his parents' death, losing an arm and a good chunk of his sanity in Vietnam. He now suffered from alcoholism and late-stage liver disease that jaundiced his skin, nails, and eyes. Nonetheless, Jimmy Junior never forsook his father's humanitarian heart and all the benefits of growing up on this island. He drank away his pain, dissolved his liver and hardened his arteries, but he never hardened his soul.

Sam felt a rush of softness towards the crumpled man. "Hey brother," offered Sam.

Jimmy Junior stirred. "Hey back," he slurred with rotted breath.

Sam jumped. Did the man just hear him? But the clearly dying Jimmy Junior was passing out again, and Sam could only watch with disbelief as Jase and Roy lifted him away from the gospel choir and over to a warm spot on the gazebo. Roy offered him some coffee and a blanket while Jase called for an ambulance. "See you on the other side!" Sam shouted out as he flew back towards Cemetery Point.

Jimmy Junior responded with a yellow grin and a feeble thumbs up. "Find me, man," he responded, and then added enigmatically, "Got somethin' to tell you..."

Mullet

• •

A recent conversation I had with a group of visitors to Cedar Key from a retirement community went something like this:

"Harvey, look! Those fish are jumping. Harv, do you see? You're not listening to me. Look up! There are fish out there, jumping!"

"Yes Bernice," came the weary reply, followed by a much perkier: "Oh wow! Look at that! They really are jumping! What kind of fish can do that?!"

"They're mullet, sir," I answered. Scientific name *Mugil cephalus*. They travel in schools according to their size. There are several theories as to why mullet jump. The main ones are that they are trying to escape from predators, are trying to remove parasites, or simply have to burn excess energy. Personally, I think they are jumping for joy!" Laughter. Others in the group began to inch closer to hear.

"Really?" exclaimed Bernice. "I didn't know that! Isn't that fascinating, Harvey?"

"Can you eat them?" asked another from the growing crowd.

I replied, "Cedar Key is actually famous for its smoked mullet dip. If there's one thing that would stop me from being a vegetarian and eating fish again, I tell you, it's that dip." The crowd laughed. I was in my groove. "But you don't want to eat mullet raw, like sashimi. Some species are safe to do that with, but not mullet." Nods and recognition. I was on fire. I offered new information: "And see all of these tiny little fish? Those are glass minnows."

"The mullet must be eating them!" guessed Harvey.

"Actually, while the Cedar Keys estuary system nurtures a vibrant food web, mullet are, in fact, vegetarians like me." The crowd let out a collective "Oh!"

The older I get, the more miraculous each and every jumping mullet—and moment—becomes. Unique, unrepeatable, and magical is this life, and so connected. The mullet invites us to just keep jumping, jumping into life, work, learning, helping, with compassion and an attitude of curiosity and discovery.

Following the path of the heart, we can jump for joy all the way.

Chapter 24

LIFE AND DEATH (2023)

SAM RETURNED TO his post at the cemetery to find things still settled and calm. There was little sound save the scuttle of a big troop of fiddler crabs sweeping across the muddy sand in the nearby marsh and the gentle melodies of a few songbirds.

The large centennial group would be coming this way soon, after morning services were finished. Emma was just arriving with Dr. Gonzalez-Tennant and Ms. Hodges. She gathered dry wood and placed it into the stone pit that she and Jase had built near Adeline's grave, using Dr. Gonzalez-Tennant's imaging to make certain that it wasn't over anyone else's. She added Spanish moss and pine cones for starter material, and lit a match.

The highly flammable pine cones and moss caught instantly, and to Sam's surprise he was jolted. Flames. Burning. Loss. *No, Emma, no. A fire ceremony is NOT what we need to do here today. Douse it!* He felt the anxiety building all around him. The Rosewood spirits had begun to panic. Their homes, their lives, all burned, all burned... No fire. *No fire!*

Emma thankfully felt it at once, and poured her water bottle over the embryonic fire. Her ceremonial traditions, while well-intentioned, didn't belong. Instead, it was the deeper, more universal practice of listening that she needed to follow. Sam slumped to the ground, relieved, waiting for the energy to calm once again.

Dr. Gonzalez-Tennant and Ms. Hodges looked at Emma

quizzically. She had to think fast. "Some of the elders, I just realized, are sensitive to fire." It was a true statement, after all. Much to her surprise, however, the anxious energy remained in the air. Sam felt it too. He looked around. The spirits were settling, even a bit curious at the gathering crowd. Some had begun to congregate around the memorial markers in the same way they had been attaching to Adeline's gravestone. The feeling wasn't from them.

I can't be gone long, he realized. *But I gotta check this out. Something's not right.*

Sam ascended and became still. He listened carefully. About a half mile away, a truck was revving its engines too loudly for this quiet Sunday morning. The revs sounded exaggerated and angry. Alarmed, he flew in that direction, not sure what he would do when he found the source.

There. Right there on 2nd street, in a big red truck parked along the curb, a large man was slugging beers and making a racket. Country music was blaring from the speakers, and when the owner of the quaint coffeehouse nearby came out to ask him to turn it down, the drunk and angry driver told him to go fuck off.

Sam realized who it was. *It's the guy Jase told me about. Clemson Dawes.*

"Sam, you gotta stop him," came a familiar voice from behind him. Sam whirled around in surprise to see his cousin Floyd floating next to Jimmy Junior, freshly dead and still grinning with yellow teeth."

"Floyd! You're back!" Sam was overjoyed to see him in coherent shape. He shifted his gaze to Jimmy Junior. "And you! The man from the park…"

"Jimmy Junior's my name," he confirmed, "proud son of Jimmy the Greek. I was heading over to my dad's gravesite and heard the ruckus, and when I found out who was causing it, I went looking for you. Really glad Floyd knew where to find you. Listen, there's something you guys need to know. Back when my dad was new to Cedar Key, folks were good to us. We had a good business selling ice cream, and everyone came to our shop, locals and tourists, black and white alike. But there was one guy, a real piece o' work, named Clarkson Dawes." Sam's eyebrows raised as he recognized the last name. "Yep," Jimmy Junior confirmed, "he was Clemson Dawes's grandad. He used to shoo off our black customers, and when we protested, he vandalized our store and called us Goombahs and Heebs. Anyways, turns out ol' Clark Dawes was the son of the man who killed YOU, Sam Carter. Clark used to talk about it all the time like it was some sorta family badge of honor. I've been listening to Clemson, Sam, and he's saying he's gonna take matters into his own hands. Saying he's gonna kill that guy that helped me last night, Roy, and burn the new cemetery signs and kill all the black folks, make Rosewood happen all over again. He's off his rocker."

Sam was stunned. The descendant of his killer, right here, inebriated and ready to....He looked in the truck and saw a shotgun and a large semiautomatic rifle in the passenger seat. *Oh my God.* Sam realized with a start that Clem Dawes might soon be headed for Cemetery Point Park. He turned to Jimmy Junior and Floyd. "Thank you both. Can y'all head back to the cemetery and keep our kin settled while the ceremony begins? I gotta deal with this guy...."

"How?" asked Jimmy Junior, still brand new to the spirit world.

"No time to teach you, Jimmy," replied Sam, "and hopefully you'll lay right to rest by your good daddy, bless his soul, so you'll never have to learn my between-world skills."

With those words, Sam swooped into the truck just as Clem floored the gas and accelerated in the direction of Cemetery Point Park.

News vehicles from all over the state were arriving at the "Newly Marked Graves" site, thanks to Jase's determination that Rosewood and African American history would get proper coverage this time. A queue of cars snaked up the hill behind the news vans and parked alongside the freshly installed memorial signs. One by one, the elders, parents and children of the seven Rosewood family branches approached, dressed mostly in black. Tourists and locals soon arrived in holiday-bedecked golf carts, watching from the periphery, while cameras and cell phones clicked busily.

Jase stepped forward, focusing the crowd's attention with his natural-born charisma as he spoke through a portable PA system. "Dear beloved family and friends, we gather here to honor our recent ancestors, who were once respected, hard-working community members of Cedar Key. A reminder that following this ceremony, we will caravan over to the cemetery of Rosewood, and similarly pay our respects. Our hope is that by uniting our deceased friends and family members, many of whom visited with each other and worshiped together between our two once-thriving communities, we will help put their souls to rest at last, so that they may rest with our love in the Kingdom of Heaven. "

The crowd replied in murmurations. "Amen!"

"Praise be."

"Friends, the century has been unkind to us. Our families have been ripped apart, our homes destroyed, our loved ones lynched and buried without ceremony. And yet, here we are in proud numbers, united in spirit and in blood, setting those wrongs right. And there are others standing with us these days, our friends and allies. Let us rejoice in thanks!" He gazed over lovingly at Roy and Emma and the supportive bands of locals and tourists interspersed throughout the crowd.

"Thank Jesus!" came a call from the crowd.

"Blessed be," came another.

Jase continued, "Let us all join hands now, and together sing 'We Shall Overcome.'"

Voices lifted up into the air and settled onto the receptive branches of the trees.

We shall overcome...

We shall overcome...

The trees opened wide, beckoning.

We shall overcome....one day....

The spirits untethered from Adeline's gravestone and the new markers, lifted by the supportive voices of their descendants and allies, and found themselves embraced.

Oh, I do believe, deep in my heart

We shall overcome...one day.

Emma felt elated. She looked over at Ma, and saw her smiling broadly, tears streaming down her pale pink cheeks. The breeze shifted, setting the leaves to trembling, Emma heard it:

Chooooooo-koooooooohhhh....

It was happening. Sam was doing it!

The voices, the trees, and the breeze were conjoined in the dance of Love, the dance that resolved any questions between life and death. Inside the cab of Clem's truck, Sam heard it too.

No one at the cemetery heard the screech of burning, oversized tires as the red truck swerved around the final turn, careening at one hundred miles per hour down the quiet, residential road where children often played. Sam had to act. Now.

"Hello, Clemson Dawes," said Sam.

Clem jumped in his seat, and looking around wildly, exclaimed, "What?! Who the hell is that?"

"I'm the man your great-granddaddy shot and killed on January 1, 1923, in Rosewood, Clem. I'm Sam Carter."

"What the FUCK?!" cried Clem. And suddenly he was crying great, dripping tears that clouded his vision and his intention. "What's happening? What the hell is happening?"

"Hurts, don't it?" continued Sam to the panicked driver. "Hurts to hear the truth, the shame. Like being pinched hard by a blue crab that won't let go. You've been taking out all that hurt inside of you on others, Clem, but I'm telling you: you don't have to anymore. We can say the truth, let the hurt and shame go, and then move on. Can you move on, Clem? Can you let it go?"

"Stop! Stop! It's too much!" Clem was full-on bawling now, and unfortunately, the surging emotion was making his foot press down harder on the gas pedal. Sam's practicing with Jase and Jimmy Junior had given him the experience to know how to talk to Clem so he could hear him, but he honestly had no idea why the man was so overcome with emotion, for god's sake. "Better slow down now, Clemson. Everything will be alright. Let's just slow down...we can talk about it....Clem.... WATCH OUT!!!"

As Clem screeched around a curve, he and Sam could see three boys who looked to be around the age of ten playing basketball in the middle of the quiet street leading to the cemetery. "SHIIIIIITTTTT!!!!!" wailed Clem as he swerved to miss them, his truck smashing through the wooden privacy fence of someone's front yard, slamming into their parked car, and flipping upside down.

We shall live in peace...
We shall live in peace...

We shall live in peace one day...

Clemson Dawes's skull was crushed. As the three young boys cautiously approached, his blood trickled in a small stream towards them. Sam quickly flew inside of his dying body, calling out to him. "Clem! Clem!" Sam viscerally felt the whole life of the man: the beatings, the violence, the shame. Clem's transitioning awareness was a lump of sobbing and suffering. Sam didn't know what to do so, reflexively, he put his hand on Clem's slowing heart. Then Sam heard himself say something that he never would have said to someone like Clem at any time before, during his life or death:

"I forgive you."

As the police cars and ambulances approached, Sam, the three boys, and just a few neighbors who had gathered heard Clemson Dawes's final words:

"I'm sorry."

Fiddler Crabs

∙∙∙

For many species, males are distinguished from females by some sort of attention-getting characteristic, such as colorful plumage, bright throats, big red buttocks, or exceptional size and strength. In the case of the fiddler crab, the impressive feature is an oversized claw, not good for much besides advertising how awesome, tough, and virile the host male obviously must be. The movement of the male's large claw to attract mates and bully smaller crabs has been compared to the frantic movements of a virtuoso violinist; hence, these easily identifiable little crabs have been given their unique moniker.

There are over one hundred species of fiddler crabs in Florida; they fall under the genus name *Uca*. The most common species found in the Cedar Keys salt marshes and mangroves is *Uca pugilator*. They are about an inch across their carapace and travel across the sandy substrate in groups that number into the thousands. Many a marsh or mangrove explorer have gasped in surprise in response to seeing a mass of crabs scuttling away from them like a moving carpet, with the males waving their harmless claws at the intruders. If the imposing human approaches any closer, the troop of crabs will slip into hundreds of holes ubiquitously dotting the sand. These holes are surrounded by thousands of tiny sand pellets, evidence of the crabs' hard work filtering the sand for algae and decomposed matter for their sustenance.

It's a good thing that fiddler crabs are so abundant, since they are a favorite food for wading birds, small mammals, and inshore fish alike. Because they have a pitifully high death rate through all stages of their one-to-two-year lifespan, females lay clutches of upwards of 15,000 eggs every two weeks all summer long. In addition to being an important food source in the salt marsh and mangrove ecosystems, these tiny mud and sand dwellers do a wonderful job of keeping the sediments well aerated via their plentiful burrows and constant movement.

Chapter 25

SAM GOES HOME (2023)

AS SAM ASCENDED from the grisly scene, he sent a prayer Clem's way and left the rest to the police, the witnesses, and the coroner. Even though he now knew how to speak directly to the living, he no longer had any more impetus to use this skill. It was time to go home.

He floated over the cemetery, watching the descendants of his kin and friends amble back to their cars while the news cameras followed from a respectful distance. The spirits were merged, and Sam relished the sense of peace that permeated the air all around him. *Good*, thought Sam. *Good*.

Drifting throughout the graves, Sam marveled at the care and resources that were poured into each family plot. Many headstones were decorated with beautiful wreaths of honor, in commemoration of the deceased's service to the United States military. *Honor*, thought Sam; *yes, that's what it's all about. It is an honor and a duty to serve in our short lifetimes, one way or another. We have so many choices: we can serve our country, each other, our planet, and equity. And maybe, just maybe, if each of us makes a choice to serve even just a little bit, balance can be restored and we bumbling, confused, suffering, beautiful humans can actually learn a thing or two and still be in the picture for many generations to come.*

He drifted towards the edges of the cemetery, noticing how the sea was already claiming the waterfront crypts. They had been carefully stabilized with rows of giant quahog shells strategically laid in cement, but accelerated sea-level rise was already dissolving the limestone and granite, breaking them into large and small chunks bit by bit. One name on a prominent tombstone half-crumbled into the rising water caught Sam's eye: *Dawes.* Just beneath the surface of the water, juvenile blue crabs picked through the rubble, looking for snacks. Stone crabs found happy new homes in the larger pieces of granite, and as they nestled in, they protruded their strong thick claws outward, ready to defend their new digs in the ruins of the gravestone.

Sam was ready. He floated over to the newly marked graves and bid a quiet farewell to cousin Floyd and his Cedar Key friends and family, now finally at peace. He watched as the last group of cars wound their way out of Cemetery Point Park, and followed them to Rosewood.

Time to go home.

Jase was waiting patiently at the front of the small Rosewood cemetery as folks arrived. He looked over at Emma; she was absorbed in a conversation with Dr. Gonzalez-Tennant about imaging Seahorse Key for unmarked Seminole graves. Roy was right next to her, holding her hand. Jase was happy for both his best friend and his cousin.

"Good to see you again, Jase," came a sultry voice from behind him. Jase turned to see Alberta Strong, the woman he'd met the last time he was in Rosewood during the soil ceremony. This time, she was dressed formally in a black, satin suit and a smart hat with a netted veil. Jase gulped. She looked beautiful.

"A-Alberta," he stuttered. "I am so glad you came. Thank you." Her smile disarmed him.

Sam watched the exchange from a few feet overhead, and couldn't resist. He drifted right into Jase's left ear and ribbed,

"Go get her, son! Use that famous Carter charm!" Jase flushed.

As the last of the attendees gathered near, Jase began by thanking the current owners of the property for access to the cemetery and the permission to do imaging of the unmarked graves along with pruning the area around the marked stones that dated from the turn of the previous century. The old headstones were brick-and-mortar reminders of a time, nearly erased, when Rosewood was a thriving community with a few hundred residents from seven families, three churches, two stores, a Masonic hall, and a school. As with the quahog-lined crypts near the shore at Cemetery Point Park, nature had begun its reclamation, but Sam wasn't offended. These folks had good lives and good support in their deaths, and now they had been long at peace, happy to return to the earth, sky, and sea. He was ready, too.

Jase shared with the crowd that the imaging that Dr. Gonzales-Tennant had done had revealed some shallow unmarked graves closer to the site of where the Rosewood homes had been; these were likely the graves of the Rosewood victims. Sam saw several areas where there were human-sized depressions in the ground: there were more than five. *How many others died unaccounted for in the massacre?*

He coasted over them. They were near the site of the Carrier house. "Sylvester? Sarah?" he queried.

He felt a stirring, a rustling of cool breeze. "Here, Sam, my old friend." He heard it from a nearby eastern red cedar tree, one so large and healthy that it had obviously escaped the sawmill. Sam approached it, but saw no one.

"Where? Who?" he asked in consternation.

"All of us, Sam. We are all here, and everywhere. We're all right. Thank you, Sam. Thank you for helping our brothers and sisters and cousins. Come home, Sam. Our time is only now, and it's infinite. Come home."

Sam pulled out his hand bones, minus one finger, and laid them gingerly beneath the roots of the century oak. As Jase invited the group to bow their heads for a moment of silence, Sam wafted over to him one last time and said, "I love you, great-grandson. Thank you. Goodbye." When Jase lifted his head, the old century oak rustled reassuringly in the cool, fresh breeze of the brand-new year.

Jase sank to his knees and finally released the lifetime of grief that he's kept in check behind decades of resilience and academic rationality. While Alberta held him, Jase's tears joined those of his ancestors, and washed the earth.

Chapter 26

EPILOGUE (2023)

ON A BALMY night in Cedar Key, when the warm breeze rustles the palm fronds under a painted sky and fiddler crabs move in scuttling murmurations among the mangroves, it's easy to imagine that you're much farther south, in the Florida Keys. The Cedar Keys were once marketed to tourists as the "Venice of the South," and have lately been compared to the Key West of one hundred years ago. But these islands are neither the Florida Keys nor Venice: they are the Islands of Cedars, *Las Islas Sabines*, a completely unique transition zone between tropical and subtropical, saltwater and fresh, the old ways of the proud and traumatized South, the much older ways of an ancient system of wisdom, beauty, and balance, and a new way of reckoning the two so that only the best parts are invited to remain.

On just such a night a couple of months after the Rosewood centennial, Jase and Roy were fishing off the Cedar Key municipal pier. Roy leaned in towards Jase, took a deep breath, and finally asked a question that had been burning at him for a very long time. "Jase, after everything we've been through together, don't you think I'm family enough by now to get in on your daddy's secret to catching monster redfish?"

Jase gave him a sly look. "Nope."

"Awww, c'mon, man!" Roy pleaded. You gotta tell me already! What is it? Bacon grease? Gizzards? You're killin' me! I have to know!"

Jase winked at Roy, then bent over the side of the pier railing and called out, "Heeeeeeere fishy fishy! Heeeeere red fishy fishy!"

Roy rolled his eyes. "Not funny man, makin' fun like.... WHAT?!" Jase's line was suddenly jumping. Jase played the reel with skill, and as the rod curved dramatically, Roy could clearly see a....monster redfish! Jase reeled it in as onlookers gathered to see the gasping grandfather red drum.

"THAT'S your secret?!" Roy exclaimed incredulously. "Saying 'here fishy fishy?'"

"Yup," Jase replied smugly, removing the hook gingerly and then, to everyone's surprise, tossing the fish back into the water.

"What'd you do that for?!" exclaimed Roy.

Jase shrugged. "We already caught plenty of fish for dinner. Wasn't his ticket yet. But now you know the family secret."

Meanwhile, Emma and Alberta sat on the other side of the pier watching the sunset. The color palette felt infinite, beyond time. "How fitting," remarked Emma, "to be sitting here under this big sky, Alberta, you and me together. About a hundred and fifty years ago, my great-great-grandma Polly Parker would have been on a boat, right about *there*...." she pointed in the general direction of Atsena Odie. "On that same day, your great-great-grandpa Dan Strong would have been working on the railroad somewhere over *there*..." she waved her arm to the east. Now, we're both right *here*, safe and happy."

"And choo-koh," whispered Roy over her shoulder, grabbing her hand. "Home." Jase and Roy had slipped up behind them, and together the four of them watched the sun bid farewell with a silence that was so bountiful, conversation would have only detracted. Roy and Jase shared a glance. *Just like when we were kids*, they said to each other without speaking a word.

An hour later, as the last of the fuschia and green faded for the night and the stars began to dance, Emma finally broke the silence. "Look!" she exclaimed, pointing behind them. The group turned to see an emphatic moon rising over the backwaters, illuminating the first lucky marsh grasses, sandbars and oyster beds with a wash of light that would eventually blanket the whole of the Cedar Keys, Rosewood, Otter Creek, Bronson, Archer, Gainesville, and way, way, beyond.

It also illuminated the remnants of the Scratch Bar, finally closed down by the health department a few weeks earlier for literally rotting in place. As the years went on, storms would sink the decaying building deep into the earth. The stand of small eastern red cedars across from the bar would grow taller as the building slowly disintegrated and fiddler crabs ventured out of their marsh and mangrove havens to pick for scraps. The jars that once lined the dusty shelves inside would be scattered all over the ground—Their glass and contents, including the yellowed bone-dust of a more-than-century-old dismembered finger—became ground into the sand to feed the trees.

hear them cry
the long dead
the long gone
speak to us
from beyond the grave
guide us
that we may learn
all the ways
to hold tender this land
hard clay direct
rock upon rock
charred earth
in time
strong green growth
will rise here
trees back to life
native flowers
pushing the fragrance of hope
the promise of resurrection

"Appalachian Elegy, Part I," bell hooks, 1952-2021, RIP

NOTE FROM THE AUTHOR

"ISLANDS OF CEDARS" is actually my second book set in Cedar Key. I wrote the first, entitled "Cedar Key," over thirty-five years ago at the age of sixteen. Its typewritten "final draft" still sits in one of the drawers in my office, because for the past three decades, I've thought about pulling out that story and working on it some more. After reviewing the a plot, which included good guys (the island residents), bad guys (the real estate developers) and the requisite hurricane that brought them all together, I found myself proud of my teenage motivation to write, and also grateful to have put some years between that first story and the more-involved and multilayered new one shared with you in this novel.

The historical events and marine biology portrayed in this novel are all factual, and I hope that readers find the book to be equal parts interesting, educational, and consciousness-raising. The main characters in this story—Jase Carter, Emateloye Tiger, Roy Bamford the Third, Clemson Dawes, and Alberta Strong—are all fictional. Likewise, the spirit version of Sam Carter and the story of both his Senegalese heritage and his descendants are fictional, as Sam Carter's actual lineage is uncertain. However, because he was the first known victim in the very real Rosewood tragedy, I was drawn to a representation of his character that would invite us to more deeply examine the past, present, and future and some of the forces that brought us to where we are today. The cemetery project led by Anna Hodges and Dr. Edward Gonzalez-Tennant from the Cedar Key Historical Society is also factual. Ms. Hodges, working with many wonderful folks like Dr. Gonzalez-Tennant, the Rosewood families and foundations, African American photojournalist Carolyn Cohen, and many others, has been tireless in her efforts to bring equity into the historical representation of our tiny little slice of old Florida paradise that is, after all, for all of us to cherish and preserve.

I learned the story of Polly Parker while working with the Seminole Tribe of Florida. I had the opportunity to spend time with former Chairman James E. Billie and other tribal members to learn the languages, history, and culture of the Tribe to enrich the elementary education programs I have developed for my "Shana Banana" children's musician persona. To me, Emateloye represents the resilience, wisdom, and compassion of mothers and mother figures everywhere, so often overlooked and underappreciated in modern society. When we learn to slow down, come out of our reactive minds and language patterns, and settle the chatter and noise around us, we begin to sense something much deeper than our usual state: an invitation to come home to our true hearts. My long-time Zen practice has accentuated this awareness, and I have found, time and again, that the ability to tap into its source is as close as the nearest tree or flicker of a breeze. Mother Nature has a powerful way of calling us Home.

For these very reasons, this book isn't just about Rosewood. I could only tell the story from my vantage point: as someone not genetically connected to any of the characters/history but blessed to be in love with the natural beauty of this part of Florida and also someone to have borne painful witness to the stories of Rosewood and race relations in northwest Florida, the Seminoles, and conflicted whites trying to navigate between their conditioned ways and a world that must transform. This book is my attempt to marry all of these elements—the descendants of Rosewood and African Americans in Cedar Key, the Seminoles, the old-school whites, and Mother Nature—to make apparent the links between them and start transforming the future.

While the details of this novel are extremely local, the story has implications that are global. Rosewood isn't just some terrible thing that happened a century ago in our little corner of the north Florida deep woods. It's a critical example of what is still happening in all sorts of ways and will happen over and over again if we do not fully acknowledge and transform it. It's not just a week in 1923; it's three hundred years prior and one hundred years since. The Rosewood massacre and events like it—the attitudes and events that make them possible and the failure to acknowledge the damage and pain and make adequate amends—will continue to have effects far into the future, across state and national boundaries. Conflict between people and damage to the planet will not end until we evolve past our old, dysfunctional patterns, refuse to tolerate bullies and oppressors, and emerge together into a new paradigm. If we don't, it will be to our peril: the rising sea will claim us, just like it's claiming the graves in the Cedar Key cemetery.

In many ways, this story and the one from my teenage years are the same in their intention. Both seek to elicit compassion and stewardship for the sacred things we are gifted at birth: our relationships, our environment, our lives, a sacred trilogy that, in truth, cannot be divided.

I hope, dear reader, that you enjoyed this story, and that you open your heart to hearing the whispers from the ethers: *Choo-koh.*

"Mama would want us to carry on."
–Evelyn Wrispus Williams
In memory of Altamese Wrispus, 1928-2021

TRIBUTE TO ROSEWOOD: "THE BLOOD"

Drip, drip, drip went the blood, in cadence with the sounds of gunfire piercing the air, crackling, then silenced with the screams of the afflicted.

Drip, drip, drip

Pooling onto the ground, forming a puddle of viscous clay cement.

Screams of terror, cries of anguish

Drip, drip, drip

Unexplainable terror gripped a community.

The sky opened up, diluting the blood, water mixing with crimson red, turning pink, before vanishing into the softened ground beneath, clay with dirt, rocks, sediment, earth.

As the blood cells give up their red pigment, the DNA slowly diffuses into the earth, as it always does when strange fruit hangs from the hardwood trees of the hammock. The blood releases cytoskeleton, cytoplasm, mitochondria, golgi bodies, ribosomes, cellulose, nuclei and the DNA genetic code of humans spilling into the earth, mixing with the genetic blueprint of the species in the hammock. Centimeter by centimeter, the DNA penetrates the top soil until it is no longer visible to the naked eye. As the earth receives its truth, it is awakened yet again by the familiar call of redemption from the dead. The dead welcome back the dust to dust. The untimely passing of blood to earth, seeping through layers of soil flowing to places unrecognizable to man, waiting for the time of full maturation.The time when maximum threshold is reached and each living tree, blade of grass, molecule of water, droplet of air, all things made of earthen resources are fully saturated with the DNA of the slain.

At maximum threshold, the blood will redeem the innocent and transform into a new creation which seeks justice for them. The blood rises to claim the fingerprint of the terrorist and seed. The life blood will see retribution and reign terror on the descendants of those who continue the unjust ways that shed innocent blood and trauma. The life blood will also provide refuge, peace, and harmony for all ready to move beyond oppression, together, into a new day of compassion and healing.

Shh, on the haloed land of the Hammock, where the earth thickens and the hammock tree grows tall, you can hear the screams of the slain demanding justice. The DNA has mutated, looking for the terrorist and unevolved descendant. The life blood is spilled throughout. The blood is bigger than their guns, their bombs, their nooses. Maximum capacity of the earth has been reached, the life blood seeks vengeance on the wickedness of man, finally providing refuge and peace to the hunted and to the helpers.

Shhh, don't you hear the slain in the Hammock of Rosewood? The DNA speaks. Be silent.

Myra Michele George (Robinson Rosewood Family Branch)
m.m.george©2022

(1) Full poem:
As I walked by
The Tree
... Cried out
Why don't you hold me anymore
Sit beneath my shade
We barely ever talk
Like we once did
100 years ago
I know
You blame me
For being
Deep inside
Us
Hidden
In the blind spot of memory
All of
Our
Pent up
Pain
We
Must Feel
I know
You blame me
Because,
If I
Had not been
They
Would not have
Dangled
Your Brother
Your Sister

Your Father
Your Mother
... From my limbs
There would be
No blood
On my branches
I would
Be
Only brown
... Like you
With green hair
Without tinge
With
No hint of red
On
My wood
Please forgive me
Had I known
If I could
... I would have
Plucked myself
Up
By
The Root!

--by E. Stanley Richardson, Poet Laureate of Alachua County FL
"Century Oak: A Conversation with a Tree"
estanleyrichardson@gmail.com

SOURCES

» Alexander, Rep. Ramon (June 12, 2021). "10 Pieces of Factual Florida History that Should be Taught in Public Schools." Tallahassee Democrat. *https://www.tallahassee.com/story/opinion/2021/06/12/critical-race-theory-10-florida-black-history-facts-teach/7651567002/*

» Barry, Savanna (March 19, 2019). "Living Shoreline Master Plan for Cedar Key." UFAS/IFAS Blogs. *https://blogs.ifas.ufl.edu/ncbs/2019/03/19/living-shoreline-master-plan-for-cedar-key*

» Bemis, Amanda (January 10, 2017). "Five Facts: Barnacles." Florida Museum. *https://www.floridamuseum.ufl.edu/science/five-facts-barnacles/*

» Bester, Cathleen (2022). "Mugil cephalus." Florida Museum. *https://www.floridamuseum.ufl.edu/discover-fish/species-profiles/mugil-cephalus/*

» Cedar Key Dolphin Project. *https://www.cedarkeydolphinproject.org/*

» Deane, Green (2018). "Cabbage Palm, Sabal Palmetto." Eat the Weeds and Other Things Too. *https://www.eattheweeds.com/cabbage-palm-sabal-palmetto/*

» Dunn, Hampton (1995). "David Levy Yulee: Florida's First U.S. Senator." University of South Florida, Sunland Tribune, Volume 21, Article 7.

»

» Fillmon, Tim (November 21, 2022). "Lynching in America/
Reconstruction-Era Lynchings in Gainesville."
https://www.hmdb.org/m.asp?m=186407

» Flank, Lenny (September 7, 2018). "Wild Florida: The
Fiddler Crab." Hidden History. *https://lflank.wordpress.
com/2018/09/07/wild-florida-the-fiddler-crab/*

» Florida Fish and Wildlife Conservation Commission.
American Brown Pelican. *https://myfwc.com/wildlifeha-
bitats/profiles/birds/shorebirdsseabirds/brown-pelican/*

» Florida Fish and Wildlife Conservation Commission.
American White Pelican. *https://myfwc.com/wild-
lifehabitats/profiles/birds/shorebirdsseabirds/ameri-
can-white-pelican/*

» Florida Fish and Wildlife Conservation Commission.
Florida Horseshoe Crab Watch-Linked with Limulus.
*https://myfwc.com/research/saltwater/crustaceans/
horseshoe-crabs/citizen-watch/*

» Friends of the Lower Suwannee and Cedar Key National
Wildlife Refuges.
https://www.friendsofrefuges.org/shell-mound-trail.html

» Gallagher, Peter (December 17, 2013). "Emateloye Estenletkvte: Polly Parker Got Away." The Seminole Tribune.
*https://seminoletribune.org/emateloye-estenletkvte-pol-
ly-parker-got-away/*

» Gonzalez-Tennant, Edward, Ph.D. Rosewood Heritage
and VR Project.
https://www.virtualrosewood.com/oral-history/

» Kaufman, Kenn (October 1, 2001). "Double-crested Cormorant." Audubon Guide to North American Birds. *https://www.audubon.org/field-guide/bird/double-crested-cormorant*

» Kennedy, Jennifer (January 24, 2018). "Southern Stingray: Dasyatis americana." ThoughtCo. *https://www.thoughtco.com/southern-stingray-dasyatis-americana-2291596*

» Key West Aquarium. "American Alligator." *https://www.keywestaquarium.com/ultimate-guide-alligators*

» Luckerson, Victor (September 10, 2020). "What a Florida Reparations Case Can Teach Us About Justice in America." Time Magazine. *https://time.com/5887247/reparations-america-rosewood-massacre/*

» Munoz, A. (2005). "Littorina irrorata" Animal Diversity Web. *https://animaldiversity.org/accounts/Littorina_irrorata/Nature Coast Biological Station. https://ncbs.ifas.ufl.edu*

» Save the Manatee Club. *https://www.savethemanatee.org/*

» ScienceDirect. "Salt Marsh." *https://www.sciencedirect.com/topics/earth-and-planetary-sciences/salt-marsh*

» Smith, Albert C. (1997). "Treasures from the Sea for Medicine." Self-published.

» Sturmer, Leslie (2007). "What's In the Clambag?" *https://shellfish.ifas.ufl.edu/clambag*

» University of Florida/IFAS Gardening Solutions (2021). "Eastern Red Cedar." *https://gardeningsolutions.ifas.ufl.edu/plants/trees-and-shrubs/trees/red-cedar.html*

» Wooten, David A. (October 1, 2020). "Trophic Ecology of Seahorse Key, Florida: A Unique Bird-Snake Interaction Network Analysis." *https://www.semanticscholar.org/ paper/Trophic-Ecology-of-Seahorse-Key*